Under Watchful Eyes

a novel

DARYLL SIMCOX

Jan-Carol Publishing, Inc

"every story needs a book"

Under Watchful Eyes
Daryll Simcox
Published February 2025
Little Creek Books
Imprint of Jan-Carol Publishing, Inc.
All rights reserved
Copyright © 2025 Daryll Simcox
Graphic Design: Tara Sizemore
Front Cover Image: © Oleg525/Adobe Stock

ISBN: 978-1-962561-63-1
Library of Congress Control Number: 2025933218

You may contact the publisher:
Jan-Carol Publishing, Inc.
PO Box 701
Johnson City, TN 37605
publisher@jancarolpublishing.com
www.jancarolpublishing.com

Once again, I would like to thank you for taking the time to read my book. UNDER WATCHFUL EYES is the second book telling of the events at Port Chatham and the encounters with the Hairy Man. The return to the port on the first anniversary of the reality television show holds many surprises for those who go ashore. I hope that you enjoy reading the book as much as I did writing it. The mythical creatures that roam the darkened forest have always intrigued me. Whether these creatures have been proven by science to exist or not, they tend to play on one's mind when alone in the woods. Thank you for reading UNDER WATCHFUL EYES. I hope it keeps you wanting to turn the page to see what happens next.

ALSO BY DARYLL SIMCOX:

The Breath of Darkness

PROLOGUE

It was just a few days shy of the one-year anniversary of the filming of the television show at Port Chatham. Nobody had visited the area since the surviving crew members and contestants boarded the boat to return home.

The cabins remained on the small hill below the old, abandoned road facing the bay. The brush and small saplings had already begun their quest to retake the area that once was cleared for the show.

The wildlife that inhabited the area continued in their daily rituals as they roamed the land, soared in the fresh mountain air, and swam in the crystal-clear waters of the bay. The leaves of the trees that bordered the shoreline would gently dance as the breeze blew across the calm waters, and small ripples would whisp across the bay, breaking up the mirrored reflection of the water. Once again, the seemingly calm area was about to be interrupted by the intrusion of a group of people investigating the events of a year ago—some wanting to go, and some who were not so keen on the idea.

CHAPTER 1

The day at the clinic had been a long one. For some reason, there had been quite a few more patients than normal. Maybe it was due to the sudden rush of pollen that had begun to fill the air, or maybe it was the fact that the weather was starting to warm up and everyone was escaping the confinements of being locked up indoors throughout the winter.

Elaine wasn't sure exactly what the reason was; she only knew that it had been a long day, and now it was time to relax. She would enjoy the Asian box meal that she had handily picked up on the way home from the small restaurant beside the grocery store. It was situated in the complex that Elaine drove by every day. The people who prepared the take-home meal were patients of Elaine's, and she was always happy to see them.

Elaine didn't mind the busy days; sometimes she would even get lost in her work enough to forget about the events they had endured nearly a year ago. But it never failed. The minute she slowed down to relax, Port Chatham and all the people involved would flood her mind. Silently, she wondered if that would ever change. Even though she never told anyone in the small community she had settled in, it would be nice to have someone to release her feelings to.

Elaine placed the contents from the boxes onto a plate and grabbed a bottled water from the fridge. She reached for the remote and turned on the television, mainly for some background noise, then she sat down at the table and began to eat. Not more than two bites later, her cell phone began to ring. Elaine looked at the number and didn't recognize it, so she simply swiped down to end the call. A couple of seconds later, the phone began to ring again. Same number, she thought. "Can't I just enjoy my food tonight?" she said aloud.

Elaine let the call forward to voicemail as she hurriedly consumed the food. Maybe she was needed by a patient, or maybe it was just another tele-marketer that had the deal of a lifetime just for her. As soon as the voicemail notification made its annoying little chime, Elaine picked up the phone and called her voicemail. As the voice from the little device began to speak, she placed her fork on the plate and stared directly at the face of the phone.

"Elaine, this is Rob Hutchins, and if possible, I would like to speak to you. If you can... Would you give me a call back at this number? Thank you."

Elaine ended the voicemail call but did not delete the message. What would Rob want to speak to her about? She hadn't spoken to the man or anyone at the network since the settlement she received after they left Port Chatham. Come to think of it, the settlement payout had come very quick-ly. It almost seemed like it was hush money to just disappear and never talk about what happened. However, the check did take care of all the debt she accumulated in her quest to become a doctor and completely paid for Elaine's relocation to where she now resided.

Elaine thought to herself, *I'm one of the lucky ones. Even with the night-mares, at least I survived. Many did not.*

She took the last couple of bites of the meal and leaned back in the chair. She stared at the phone until the last drop of water in the bottle was con-sumed. Hesitantly, Elaine picked up the phone and punched in the numbers.

Somewhere between the second and third ring, she heard, "Hello, this is Rob Hutchins."

Elaine paused just a second, then said, "Rob, this is Elaine... How can I help you?"

Rob responded, "Thanks for returning my call, Elaine. I wasn't quite sure if you would consider it or not. There's something I would like to discuss with you. It seems that a lot of interest has developed in the last couple of months, and I was wondering if you would be willing to help me out."

Elaine asked, "Helping how?"

Rob replied, "They're going back, Elaine. There are some people—"

Elaine interrupted, "Wait a minute, Rob, who's going back and why?"

"Listen, the network and the insurance company want to investigate to determine just exactly what took place at the port last year. Plus, they want to extract the remains of the others so the families can have closure," replied Rob.

Elaine said sternly, "I understand going after the others. I argued with you people about that right after we left. But what do you mean they want to determine exactly what took place? For crying out loud, Rob, we gave them a detailed description of everything."

Rob answered, "I know, Elaine, but the network and the insurance company are really starting to apply pressure. I'm not totally sure what this is all about."

"Rob, are you asking me to go back?"

Rob hesitated for just a second. "Yes, Elaine."

Elaine paused, then responded, "I'm not really the least bit interested, Rob. I think one vacation to the port will last me a lifetime."

"Please, Elaine," Rob pleaded. "I need for some of you guys to go back with me."

"You're going?" Elaine asked.

"Yes."

"Need to save your rear end, Rob?" Elaine asked.

Rob shook his head. "It's not my rear end I'm worried about, Elaine."

"What are you talking about?" Elaine asked.

Rob described all the details of the expedition to Elaine—how the network and the insurance company were pressuring all involved in the show. He explained how they were supposed to hire the same captain to take them back to the port, but this time they would sleep on the boat instead of the cabins. The network had hired four men to be the bodyguards for everyone while they searched for the remains of the others. Rob said, all in all, there would be nine people going ashore, plus any of the original group he could talk into going back.

After Rob finished talking, Elaine asked, "And just how many of the original group are going?"

Rob answered, "The only one who will commit is Shelley. Mark and Willy said no. As a matter of fact, they plainly told me not to ever call them again. Ronnie listened to basically the same spiel I just gave you and politely said he just wasn't interested, but I think he may be on the fence."

"Why is any of us going back really that important, Rob?" Elaine asked. "None of us know of the whereabouts of the others. For Pete's sake, if anybody should go back, it would be Mark. At least he knows the location of Mr. Long."

Rob replied, "Mark gave a detailed description of Mr. Long's location before he hung up. Plus, it is in his report. But the reason I need you people to go is the bond you developed with the creature."

Elaine raised her voice, "Bond? Are you kidding me, Rob? We were lucky to get out alive. I admit we somehow won the favor of these creatures, simply because they let us survive. I'm not sure if I would trust this so-called bond enough to go back."

Then, Rob said, "Elaine, listen to me... I'm thinking that at least two and maybe all four of these so-called bodyguards are not quite as interested in protecting us as they are in killing one of the creatures."

"What?" Elaine yelled into the phone.

"I overheard discussions after the last meeting coming from down the hall. I'm thinking they are simply going to bag one of the creatures."

"Call Shelley and get both of us tickets to Arizona," Elaine said. "Is that where Ronnie is still living?"

Rob simply replied, "Yes."

Then, Elaine added, "Shelley and I will meet at the airport, then we will talk to Ronnie. Hopefully, you will have to buy three tickets to Alaska."

Rob smiled and said, "I'll call Shelley as soon as I hang up, and when I've made the arrangements, I'll let you know. And... Thanks, Elaine."

***

At 10 minutes past eleven o'clock the next day, Elaine stepped off the airplane and walked into the terminal. She wasn't sure if she or Shelley were the first to arrive. As Elaine was surveying the inside of the airport, she heard a familiar voice shouting her name. Directly to the left of her was Shelley holding the handle of her roll-along travel case. After an exchange of hand waves, Elaine made her way to Shelley. They immediately hugged each other and began to make their way to the baggage pick-up area. Once there, they stood patiently watching for Elaine's luggage, even though Shelley had no earthly idea what it looked like. Finally, Elaine spotted the tan bag arriving on the conveyor.

Elaine pointed and said, "There it is. No lost luggage so far."

"Could we talk a bit before we go see Ronnie?" Shelley asked.

Elaine responded, "I think that would be a wise thing. We need to have our ducks in a row before we get to his house."

The two of them made their way to the rental car counter, picked up the keys for the car that Rob had reserved, and in just a couple of minutes were making their way through the parking lot. Finally, Shelley spotted the burgundy sedan. "There it is, Elaine. How about you drive?"

Elaine replied, "Sounds good to me. We'll have to GPS the address and hope it leads us to where we need to go."

They unlocked the car and placed the luggage in the trunk. As they sat down on the leather seats and closed the doors, Shelley reached over and placed her hand on Elaine's forearm. Shelley stared into Elaine's eyes and asked, "Do you think this is a wise decision? I have trouble sleeping most of the time. Even when I'm awake, it all runs through my mind."

Elaine turned to look out the window. "I have nightmares too, Shelley, and most days it's in my thoughts even as I work. I think about it constantly. I told Rob that I wasn't interested in going back... That is, until he mentioned the possible motives of the bodyguards."

Shelley adjusted herself in the seat. "Yeah, that kinda persuaded me also. Plus, it's really laid heavy on my mind about the others. They need to come home."

Elaine said, "I agree, and Rob says he's going ashore with us. I'm sure he has some feelings of responsibility for not just us, but especially for the ones that were left behind."

Shelley shook her head. "Yes, I believe he does. Let's go talk to Ronnie and see just exactly what he thinks."

Elaine punched in the address on the GPS, and almost immediately the information came up on the screen. They pulled out of the parking lot and started toward the location provided for Ronnie's residence.

***

Back in the large conference room at the network building, Rob was leaning back in the comfortable chair. He was staring at the table while gently tapping his lips with one of the company pens. Rob was trying to choreograph in his mind all the required steps to get everyone back at the port. Really the only thing left was to purchase the correct number of airline tickets for the people from last year. In his mind, he dearly hoped that Elaine and Shelley could convince Ronnie to join them. That would guarantee Rob that at least three sane people would accompany him on this trip.

Suddenly, the door to the conference room opened, and nine people funneled into the room in single file. All found a seat around the table and sat down. The last to enter the room, whom Rob recognized as one of the vice presidents of the company, closed the door and seated himself at the head of the table.

The vice president began to speak, "As everyone is aware... Nearly a year ago, we experienced a catastrophic situation in the filming of a show. Nobody is trying to point a finger at any one person; however, we have reason to believe that the story of Port Chatham is about to hit the airwaves. As a corporation, we will take full responsibility for all that took place. We have contacted the families of the people left behind at the port and informed them we are going back with a team to retrieve their loved ones. Rob, I believe this is no different than some of the reality shows we have produced in the past, and the company is not holding you responsible, but I do believe it is important for you to be part of the team. I appreciate that you volunteered to return and play an important role in this search operation."

The vice president then nodded at Rob and began to introduce the team members. First, he recognized the two gentlemen from the insurance company that represented the network: "These two gentlemen are Jeff Sizemore and Aaron Nelson from the insurance company. Next, we have Joe Wilburn and Whitney Moore representing the network, and these four men will serve as guards as the team searches for the others."

Then, the vice president pointed to the four men sitting side by side and asked them to introduce themselves. One by one, they raised their hand and told the group their names. First was Brad Easton, then Wilson Wilkins. Next was Harold Birchfield, and lastly was David Felder.

Then, the vice president stood up and addressed the group, "You nine will be going ashore to retrieve the others from a year ago, plus some of the original group from last year will accompany you. Please be careful. Let's just get in there and get out, okay?"

Everyone nodded and slowly rose from their chairs. They began to file out of the room, and Rob stared at the four so-called guards that would protect them. He could now confirm in his own mind after hearing them introduce themselves that, indeed, these were the men he overheard discussing the port earlier. Rob knew for a fact that some or all of them had a different motive for going with them; it wasn't just protection and closure for the families of the others. He was skeptical of the arrangement that the network had made with these men, and he knew good and well he was the fall guy for all that had happened. As Rob exited the room, he stared at the team as they walked down the hallway to the elevator, and silently he hoped Shelley and Elaine could persuade Ronnie to join them. They might need all the help they could get.

CHAPTER 2

The drive from the airport to Ronnie's address had taken nearly 40 minutes for Elaine and Shelley. They didn't really mind the journey, for it had given them time to discuss their feelings from the previous year. At one point, Shelley told Elaine that she had really needed to talk to someone about the port but was always afraid to. She felt like outsiders just wouldn't understand. She mentioned that there were a couple of close family members that she confided in, but the only one who truly understood was her cousin, who had the encounter while hunting back in Louisiana. Shelley said they would get together from time to time, and he would sit and listen to her vent about the experiences at the port. He never tried to solve any of the issues she was having. Mostly, he would only interject when she asked a question, but he was a great listener.

Elaine expressed her feelings about keeping everything inside. She told Shelley her move to the small community was to try and start fresh. The only issue was that there was nobody there for her to talk to. They only knew her as the doctor at the clinic; nobody knew about the things that had taken place prior to her arrival in their small town. Elaine told Shelley there were pros and cons about her situation, and she reiterated her love for being a doctor and the patients she took care of. Then, Elaine turned to Shelley and told her that she envied her for having someone to talk to.

Suddenly, the voice from the GPS device interrupted the women: "Take a right at the next intersection. Your destination is on your left... 2021 Harrison Drive."

After making the right turn, Shelley spotted the number above the door of a ranch-style brick house. She said, "There, Elaine. 2021 Harrison Drive."

The two women turned into the driveway, and Elaine parked the car beside a red SUV in front of the garage door. Elaine looked at Shelley and smiled. "Well, here we are. Let's go talk to Ronnie."

They walked up the sidewalk to the front door, and Shelley reached out and pressed the doorbell button. Each of them heard the chimes on the opposite side of the door. They patiently waited for someone to answer. The large white door that had the welcome sign in the upper center section opened, and Shelley and Elaine were met with the wide smile that was on Ronnie's face.

Ronnie said, "Well, my, my. Somehow I kinda figured that I would be seeing you girls, especially since Rob said he needed some of us to go back. Come on in, ladies."

Shelley and Elaine grinned at Ronnie as he stepped back and motioned for them to enter. They walked into the living room, and Ronnie closed the door. "Would you gals like some water or maybe an iced tea?"

Shelley turned and chuckled. "Not me, I'm fine."

Elaine said, "Me neither, thanks."

Ronnie then asked, "So, what brings you ladies all the way out to Arizona? On a joint vacation, or am I right about Rob and going back?"

"No vacation," Shelley said. "Guess it's your second guess."

Ronnie clinched his lips and stared at the two of them. "That's what I figured. You two really going back?"

Elaine took a deep breath. "We've got to, Ronnie. We need to bring the others back, plus we need to ensure that nothing happens to the creatures that live there."

Ronnie tilted his head to the left. "The same creatures that killed the others?"

"Yes," Shelley said.

Ronnie placed one hand into his other hand and responded, "I don't know, people. I've spent the better part of the last year trying to forget about that port and what took place. I don't know if I could even mentally convince myself to go back."

Shelley turned, and she walked to the couch and sat down. Her eyes focused on the two books lying on the coffee table. She pointed to the books and said to Ronnie, "Judging from your reading material sitting here, it doesn't appear like you're trying to forget at all. Looks to me like you are studying our friends at the port. Doesn't quite look like you are attempting to wipe your mind clear of them."

Ronnie smiled. "Yeah, one would think, but those were bought by my wife. Seems she has become quite the enthusiast since our little adventure, and after I opened up about what happened in North Carolina with that thing on the mountain."

Shelley asked, "She didn't know about North Carolina?"

"No, until telling you people, Mom and Dad were the only ones that knew," Ronnie replied. "Them and the other kids. I don't know who the other boys told the story to, but after hearing one of the boys tell a classmate and having that guy laugh at us, I just kept my mouth shut."

"Nobody is laughing now," Elaine said. "We all know they are real...and they may need our help, Ronnie."

Ronnie looked away, then turned back to Elaine. "Don't you remember how powerful those things were? There were fourteen of us on that mountainside, supposedly thirteen of which had the safety of the cabins. We had three guns, and I'm sure Mr. Long was well prepared, and everything still went wrong."

Shelley asked, "Did it really go wrong? After all, we were the ones that infringed on their territory and way of life." Then, she added, "We were the ones that caused the problem; all they wanted to do was exist in the same manner that they have for who knows how long."

Ronnie replied, "Exactly. I feel really bad for the families of the people who were left behind, but do you think we need to invade their privacy again?"

Just then, they heard a car pull into the driveway. Next was the sound of a door shutting. "That would be my wife returning from her shopping spree with her best friend," Ronnie said.

Ronnie walked to the front door and opened it. As his wife entered the house, he smiled and said, "Only one bag? The ole checking account is smiling today."

Ronnie's wife laughed, and she walked over to a cream-colored chair and placed the department store bag onto it. "You didn't tell me we were having company today, Ronnie," she said. "That's kind of rude, you know."

Ronnie pointed to Elaine and Shelley. "These two kinda caught me off guard. Alicia, dear, this is—"

Alicia interrupted, "Elaine and Shelley. It's nice to meet you ladies. I've heard all about you."

"I hope it wasn't all bad," Shelley said.

Alicia chuckled. "Not one bad thing. Ronnie said you were two of the bravest women he had ever met. So, tell me, girls, are you going back?"

"Yes," Elaine said.

Alicia looked at Ronnie, and then back at Elaine. "Do you think they would let me go?"

"Honey..." Ronnie began.

Alicia interrupted, "Come on, Ronnie. I've been studying these things ever since you got home, and I want to see that place."

Ronnie turned and walked to the entrance to the kitchen. He placed his hand on the door. "I'm afraid for anyone to go back to that place, but especially you. You don't have a stone, Alicia."

"You still got your stone, Ronnie?" Shelley asked.

Alicia answered for him, "Yep, and he never leaves home without it."

Ronnie added, "It sounds stupid, but I had a local man make me a little leather case for it, almost like a phone case. I carry that rock everywhere I go, even to the grocery store. Might be a Hairy Man hiding out at the meat section, you know."

Everyone laughed, then Shelley lifted her shirt just barely above her waist. "Something like this case?"

Ronnie smiled, and Elaine pulled out the chain that supported the stone that the creature presented to her in the cabin. "Carry it always," Elaine said with a smile.

Alicia put her hands on her hips and looked at Ronnie. "Ronnie, I want a stone."

The four of them sat at the dining room table with four glasses of iced tea. The three re-lived their experience at the port, while Alicia soaked in every word. She had the wonder in her eyes of a kid in a candy store. In her mind, she was hoping that Elaine and Shelley could somehow convince her husband to return to the port. After about an hour, Shelley finally asked Ronnie again about the trip. He replied that Alicia really wanted to see the place, and if they could convince Rob to let her tag along with them, then he would return. Ronnie turned to Alicia and firmly pointed his index finger at her. He said, "We'll both go, but you have to stay on the boat, agree?"

Alicia smiled. "Whatever you say, dear."

Elaine removed her cell phone and punched in Rob's number; he answered as though he was sitting at a desk just expecting the phone to come to life. Elaine informed Rob that Ronnie was on board, but only if his wife could go also. She sternly told Rob that he was going to need all three of them to return to the port, so he'd better make Alicia part of the team, or they would all cancel. Rob paused for a second and then said he would call her right back. Elaine smiled and told Rob they were going to grab a bite to eat, but she would be waiting for his call. Elaine grinned as she looked around the table at the others. "That was pretty much Hollywood material there, wasn't it?" she said.

Everybody laughed, and Shelley slid her chair back and stood. "Let's go eat, people, and we'll let Elaine handle ordering the food."

The four sat for just a minute, deciding on the type of restaurant they would be heading to, then they exited the house and started down the concrete sidewalk bordered by the neatly kept flowerbed. Ronnie asked if they wanted him to drive, but Elaine vetoed the suggestion. She told Ronnie they would take the rental; this tab was on Rob and the network. However, Elaine did make Ronnie sit in the front passenger seat to direct the group in the correct direction, and the four chatted all the way to the restaurant.

***

Back at the network, Rob approached the secretary to the vice president and kindly asked if he was available to speak to. The secretary buzzed the vice president and informed him that Rob Hutchins was here to see him. Thirty seconds later, Rob closed the door to the luxurious office and began to plead his case for the group, inviting Ronnie's wife along for the trip. Finally, he told the VP that if they didn't allow her to tag along with Ronnie, the entire group was going to back out. The conversation bounced back and forth for a few minutes, then the VP made a call. After a few "yes, sirs" and a couple of nods in Rob's direction, he ended the call.

He looked at Rob and shook his head. "I hate the fact that we got to go back at all, Rob." He produced what one might consider a small smile and continued, "You can tell the group that Alicia can go along. But for Heaven's sake, Rob, try to make her stay on the boat."

Rob said, "Okay," and stood from the large leather chair. He began to walk toward the door when the VP spoke once again.

"Hey, Rob, be careful up there." Then, the vice president rose from his chair and approached Rob. "Listen... I'm not trying to make you the fall guy for what happened last year. I don't think anybody around here is."

Then, he leaned toward Rob and lowered his voice. "I think this whole deal is the network trying to save face and pretending to be the good guy, but even I'm not allowed to be part of certain discussions. I do know these network people who are going, and they are really good individuals as far as I know, but one can never be sure of the pressure that can be applied to human beings. The two representing the insurance company and the four so-called bodyguards, I know absolutely nothing about, so you guys pay attention at all times. Okay?"

Rob nodded and left the room. Then, he traveled down the hallway and got on the elevator, four floors down, and Rob walked through the lobby to the outside air. He made his way to one of the benches surrounding a small fountain, removed his phone, and called Elaine.

***

Shortly after ordering their meals at the steakhouse, the salads had arrived for the four guests. They were halfway through eating when Elaine's phone began to ring. Immediately, she looked at the face of the device and saw it was Rob. Elaine answered the call, and within seconds began to smile at the others. At one point, she even gave the group a thumbs-up signal.

Elaine ended the call and sat her fork down in the salad bowl. She told everyone that Alicia was formally invited on the cruise to Port Chatham. She informed them that Rob would make all the arrangements and call back with the details—all they needed to do was get Ronnie and Alicia home to pack after they finished at the restaurant. Then, Elaine said there was no rush, though it would probably be tomorrow morning at the earliest for them to get a flight out.

17

CHAPTER 3

E arly the following morning, Ronnie and the three ladies boarded the first of the planes for their journey from Arizona to Alaska. In his mind, Ronnie was already questioning their decision to return to the port, but he didn't want to dampen the excitement that Alicia was already exhibiting to the others. As they took their assigned seats, Ronnie couldn't help but think if she had been at the port a year ago, she might not be so giddy about it now. He knew that not only did he have to look after himself, but also now he had to guard the woman he had loved for so many years. Not to forget Shelley and Elaine either. He was the only man returning from a year ago, and he felt a responsibility to them also. Each of them sat back, fastened their seatbelts, and readied themselves for the first leg of the adventure.

Alicia placed her hand on Ronnie's, and as he looked over at her, she winked and smiled. Ronnie forced himself to smile back and turned back forward as the plane began to taxi. Within a couple of minutes, the plane was airborne, and the four of them were on their way to Alaska.

***

The group that had been assembled by the network were well on their way to the small airport they would be landing in once they got to Alaska. Then, there would be a small ride to where the captain of the boat from last year was waiting on their arrival. Rob Hutchins sat at a window and peered at the white fluffy clouds as they flew by them. They gave the appearance of giant cotton balls floating in the vast sky. He wondered just exactly what was in store for the group once the captain got them to the port. Everybody on the flight had pretty much kept to themselves. There was the occasional conversation, but it was nothing pertinent to the trip. Mostly, only complaints about the plane or how uncomfortable the seats were. There was no talk about how they would approach the situation they were headed into.

Rob thought back to the last visit he had with the VP in his office. Why did he get close, and why did he whisper at the end of the conversation? Did the VP know more than he was telling Rob, or was he really in the dark on some things? *After all*, Rob thought, *he did genuinely show a real concern for our safety.* Rob decided to try and not read too much into the meeting, but he knew for sure that he wanted to talk to the captain of the boat and the returning group alone.

Suddenly, the captain spoke over the intercom and informed the passengers they would be arriving at the destination in about fifteen minutes, and the FASTEN YOUR SEATBELTS light illuminated at the front of the cabin. After fastening his belt, Rob returned to looking out the window. It was hard to believe how majestic the view was; it was exactly as he remembered it from nearly a year ago. After a slightly bumpy descent, the wheels of the plane touched down on the runway, then it taxied to a small building that represented a hangar more than a terminal.

A small-statured, round man exited the side door and approached the plane. After the turbo-prop engines shut down, the door of the plane was opened, and the passengers began to exit the plane. The nine people on this first flight allowed the three passengers that were not of their party to exit first, then one by one, they stepped out into the fresh Alaskan air and took a deep breath. Everyone followed the small, round man to the terminal door and entered the building. Rob watched the three anonymous passengers simply walk through the building and pass through the door on the opposite side. He concluded that they had made this trek before, and someone was probably waiting on them in the parking lot.

The man from the small airport turned and faced the group. He informed them that two vans were outside, and as soon as the group's luggage was loaded, they would be on their way to the boat. Then, he told everyone to relax while they unloaded the plane, and he walked back through the door they all had just entered. The two from the network and the two from the insurance company all found chairs, and they made themselves as comfortable as they could in the folding metal seats. The four bodyguards wandered over to a large window and stood staring at the surrounding mountains. Rob slowly turned and walked through the door to approach the guys unloading the plane. They were methodically placing all the items on rusty old roll carts and taking them around the side of the building.

As two younger boys pushed the last of the carts away from the plane, the man from the airport turned to face Rob and said, "That's the last of it. As soon as they get it in the vans, you guys will be on your way."

Rob asked the man, "How long before the second group gets here?"

The man informed Rob that it would be about three and a half hours, but they had their own vans to be transported in.

Then, Rob asked, "Would it be alright if I waited on them here?"

The small man nodded and said that would be fine; he was welcome to wait in the office till they arrived. Rob told the man if it was possible, he would like to call the captain of the boat and talk to him before the others arrived. The man looked at Rob and slightly raised his eyebrows. Rob said it was nothing major—he just wanted to touch base with him. The man nodded and told Rob that when the others departed, he would summons the captain on the radio. Both men walked back into the small terminal, and the man from the airport told the others they were loaded and ready to go. Rob informed the group that he was going to wait on the previous contestants and accompany them once they arrived.

Rob took a seat in one of the hard metal chairs as the other eight followed the man from the airport through the side door and climbed into the two vans. The four bodyguards loaded up in one of the vans, and the other four slid onto the worn bench seats of the second one. In just a matter of minutes, the vans exited the small pothole-filled parking lot and started down the road. When the man returned inside, he walked up to Rob and extended his hand. "Conley's the name," he said. "What's yours?"

Rob took the man's hand. "Rob Hutchins, sir."

Conley smiled. "There's no 'sir' in my name, Rob."

Both men chuckled, and Conley said, "Let's see if we can get ole Captain Frank to answer the radio."

Rob grinned. "Sounds good, but that's kinda odd... All I ever remember calling him last year was 'Captain.'"

Conley responded, "Mostly that's all anybody ever calls him. He's known around these parts as the Old Captain. He pretty well paid his dues with the seas, I suppose."

Rob asked, "Does he ever talk about last year and what happened at the port?"

Conley answered, "Not to my knowledge. You see, Rob, most people don't talk about that place. Not about last year, not about the fishing settlement, not about any time in between. I suppose some folks may talk about it behind closed doors. I know I have, but for the most part it is never talked about or visited. If someone goes there, they never go ashore. There's been a few cases of people venturing onto the land around Port Chatham, but they never came back."

"When we were getting the show together, we thought that was just some sort of hocus-pocus stuff."

Conley tilted his head slightly. "Yeah... Well, what do you think now?"

Rob mimicked Conley's head gesture. "Now, I know better."

Conley lifted his arm slightly and motioned for Rob to follow him. They walked to the side of the room facing the runway and turned to the door situated in the back corner of the room. Conley turned the knob and opened the door. As they walked into the small room, Rob noticed the radios and the weather monitoring equipment all crammed onto a small rack sitting above a desk that obviously had been around for a long time. Conley took notice of Rob as he studied the equipment and the room's surroundings. When Rob noticed he was being watched, he turned to the large window and glanced at the runway outside.

Conley smiled and said, "Mr. Hutchins, I guess the control room really ain't what one might be used to down in other parts of the country, but I assure you, it perfectly serves our purpose up here. You must realize that this place is, as we like to call it, the end of the line. But we manage quite well. We helped get you here, and we will get you guys out."

Rob responded, "I am not doubting you or the capabilities of the facility. Last year, I simply passed through the building and loaded into the van. I guess this time, I have a little more on my mind."

Conley tilted his head again, but this time in the opposite direction. "And just what's on your mind, Rob?"

Rob replied, "I'm not too sure this trip is a good idea. I firmly believe that what the survivors told us about what transpired last year was the absolute truth. I also have some reservations about those people that just left in the two vans. I think they may be here for other reasons than that of recovering the remains of the people who were left behind. I would greatly appreciate it if you wouldn't mention that to anyone, Conley."

Conley sat down at the desk. "Don't worry, Rob. Up here, we are well known for keeping a tight lip. I won't mention anything you don't want me to."

"Thanks, Conley," Rob said. "No offence, but I'm already looking forward to that part of you getting us out of here."

Conley laughed, "Don't like our little vacation getaway, Rob?"

"Oh, I love it here. Just curious about what awaits us at the port."

Conley rose from his chair and walked over to a small table. He poured Rob and himself a cup of coffee. He handed the cup to Rob and pointed to the jar of sugar sitting beside the pot. Rob took the white plastic spoon lying on a folded paper towel and added two scoops of sugar to his coffee. After stirring the contents of the cup, he wiped the spoon with another paper towel and returned the spoon to its rightful place.

Conley walked back to the desk and sat down in the worn leather chair. Rob followed and took the position of standing on his right side. Conley dialed up the frequency on the old radio that sat on the far right of the equipment shelf, then he began to summon Captain Frank as Rob studied the lights on the front of the device.

Suddenly, the response came back from the radio: "Well, hello there, Conley. How you been, ole buddy?"

Conley turned to Rob and winked. "Doin' pretty good, Captain, just wanted to give you a little heads up. The first of the group have just left the airport and are now enjoying the scenic tour ride to your facility."

Captain Frank laughed, "Wonderful. I can't wait to show them the luxurious vessel they will be sailing on for their cruise."

Rob smiled. He could imagine the expression on the captain's face. "Captain, it's good to hear your voice again," Rob said.

Captain Frank asked, "Well, my, my, how you doin', Rob? And why ain't you on the van tour to my facility?"

Rob answered, "I wanted to wait on the others from last year, Captain."

"And how many are coming back, Rob?" Captain Frank asked.

"Three, plus Ronnie's wife."

"Nobody ever gave us the exact number," Captain Frank said, "but I think we got plenty of room on the boat."

Then, Rob said, "Do me a favor, Captain... Be careful of what exactly you say to the first group when they arrive. I don't know these individuals, and I think there could possibly be more to this little trip than search and rescue. When the others arrive, we'll be right over to your facility as soon as we can, and if possible, I would like to speak to you in private."

Captain Frank said, "Not a problem, Rob, and don't worry. I'll just be my ole cheerful self to the others when they get here."

All three men chuckled, and Conley told Captain Frank it would be about three hours when the second plane would arrive. Then, he assured the captain that he and his helpers would have them on their way as soon as possible.

After the radio conversation ended, Conley turned and smiled at Rob. He told him to make himself as comfortable as possible and enjoy all the coffee he so desired. After all, it was a free service that the airport offered to all the visitors of the area. Rob thanked him and walked to the small table to get a refill. This time, he only added one teaspoon and stirred it to the desired color. Rob stared at the contents of the cup and thought back to the time in the control room when Captain Frank added his own special ingredient to his own cup. They were concerned with the approaching storm that was headed for the port and the effect it was going to have on the participants. He remembered worrying about the effect it might have on the show's outcome. They had no idea what the participants would encounter, and they certainly never dreamed there would be loss of life. Perhaps the captain's special sauce would be a perfect fit for the cup he now held in his hand. Maybe Captain Frank knew a little more than just about the sea. Did he know more about Port Chatham than he disclosed last year?

Rob walked to the window and studied the surroundings of the small airport; how could such a beautiful place have turned into the disaster it was last year? He wondered what the families of the ones who didn't survive thought of him. Rob was pretty sure the network had put his name to the forefront of each conversation with the family members. In a way, they were right, though. The entire thing had been Rob's idea, and he'd had a lot of sleepless nights because of it. A lot had changed for Rob in the last year. After the failure of the show, his wife suddenly decided to leave him, which only added to the feelings of failure he had experienced. But now, he felt a deep obligation to the families to bring their loved ones home. It was the right thing to do, and he felt it was his responsibility to see it carried out properly. Rob also felt there was more; it was also his responsibility to protect the creatures that inhabited the port, Elaine sure got excited when he mentioned the possible motives of the bodyguards. Shelley didn't hide her feelings either when he talked to her on the phone. Had he made a mistake telling them about the guards? Rob wondered if he had once again put the survivors into a dangerous situation. Maybe they would have returned anyway. Possibly, they didn't think any more of him than the other families, or even his ex-wife. Rob figured it wouldn't take long to decipher their opinions once they arrived.

Rob wandered over to the leather chair at the equipment table and sat down. He placed his hands in his lap and leaned back. The journey to the airport had been a long one. Now, the physical and mental fatigue were beginning to set in. Rob just needed to rest for a while. He closed his eyes, and in just a couple of minutes, Rob faded off to sleep.

Rob awoke to someone shaking his shoulder. He jumped and sat straight up in the chair. Quickly, he remembered where he was and who was trying to awaken him. Rob felt like he had just dozed off until his eyes focused on the hands of the clock hanging on the wall. He had been asleep for quite some time.

Conley said, "Sorry to bother you, Rob, but your friends will be arriving shortly. Can I steal your seat for a bit?"

Rob rose from the chair. "Yes, sir, sorry about that, Conley. Here you go."

Rob stood and moved to the window as Conley began to communicate with the pilot of the incoming plane. He could see what he believed to be the aircraft coming over the mountain range that surrounded half of the area. Within minutes, the plane was on approach, and Rob watched intently as it touched down on the runway. Then, it taxied up to the building, and after a few minutes, the pilot shut down the engines.

Conley placed his hands on the chair's armrests and stood. "Well, let's go welcome your friends."

CHAPTER 4

As the two men exited the building and approached the plane, Rob immediately noticed the plane to be smaller than the one they flew in on. He realized why it looked so small as it came into view over the mountains. The boys that worked at the airport quickly placed the blocks under the wheels to keep the plane in its rightful spot. After a minute, the door was opened, and everyone was assisted down the steps where they were met by Conley and directed toward the office building. Rob walked ahead of the group and held the door as the four members of the group entered. Rob turned to look at Conley, who motioned to him that he would be there shortly. Rob then realized that Conley was honoring the time he had asked for to be alone with the group.

Rob closed the door behind him and faced the others. "I really appreciate you guys coming back. I know this is a difficult position I've put you in."

Shelley scanned the room. "Where's the rest of them?"

Rob answered, "They've already loaded into vans and are on their way to meet the captain... Listen, people, I'm not exactly sure how you feel about me. Whatever your feelings are, I understand. I feel it's very important that the other families get closure, but I feel even more strongly about protecting these creatures and their habitat."

Elaine took a step in Rob's direction. She said, "We explained everything that happened in complete detail; nobody left anything out or told a single thing that wasn't the absolute truth."

Rob looked Elaine directly in the eye. "I know that, and you certainly know that. But I'm not exactly sure about all this, and I'm definitely not sure about the members in the vans already on the road. I feel sure that it has been a rough year for all of us, and I am positive that the events of last year will follow us for the rest of our lives."

Shelley walked to the large plate glass window facing the parking lot. "You weren't there, Rob. I have nightmares even when I just doze off watching TV. It's always on my mind in some form or fashion."

Rob dropped his head and said, "Maybe I would understand better if I had been at the cabins, Shelley. My nightmares consist of the fact that this whole thing was my idea and that it's my fault that these people lost their lives. A lot of loved ones didn't get to come home to their families, and I bear the responsibility of that situation."

Ronnie shifted on his feet. "What about the network? Do they hold you responsible?"

Rob answered, "Well, they say they don't, but everyone knows how that works... Somebody must be the fall guy. But that's okay. I really don't care what they think, I just want to do what's right and get out of here."

Shelley turned from looking out the window. "What does your family think? They're supporting you, right?"

Rob slightly adjusted his posture, and after a couple of seconds he began to speak, "My wife left about six months ago. I'm not sure if it's because I failed at the network or if it was my drinking and depression that finally made up her mind to hit the road. Whatever it was, there's no reason to worry about it now. The main thing is to recover the others and protect these creatures."

Just then, the door to the runway swung open, and Conley announced to the group, "Just a few more minutes, and we'll have you guys on the road." Rob introduced everyone to Conley, and he politely acknowledged each one of them. When Rob introduced Ronnie's wife, he informed him that she was the newcomer for the little expedition to the port. Ronnie was quick to add that she was the only reason he decided to return. Alicia walked over to Conley and smiled. She reached out her hand, and Conley quickly accepted the gesture. Alicia told Conley it was a privilege to meet him, and she appreciated his help with all their bags. Conley nodded to her and told her it was his honor, but before he dropped her hand, he looked Alicia sternly in the eyes and said, "You be careful, lady."

Then, Conley turned to the group. "In fact, all you guys be careful at that place. The locals don't visit the port. Mostly nobody even talks about that place. Some of you have already met the things that live there, and you know them to indeed be real. Don't push your luck."

"Conley, I got a question," Rob said.

"What's that?" Conley asked.

Rob had a puzzled look on his face. "Why weren't there any discussions about the port when we got the show together last year?"

Conley sat in one of the old metal chairs. "We did raise concerns, but the group that came up to build the cabins wouldn't listen. They mostly laughed and made light of what the captain and I explained to them. After they finished their work and came back through the airport on their way home, I heard a couple of them making jokes about the boogeyman. I think they just flat out got lucky, Rob."

The door to the parking lot opened, and one of the young boys informed Conley that the van was loaded. The group walked through the door while the young worker held it open for them. Conley followed and closed the van door as everyone began to position themselves on one of the three bench seats. After all were safely buckled into their rightful seat, he slapped the window of the van and waved. Next, he silently moved his lips and told everyone to be careful. It was obvious that Conley was concerned as he turned to walk back into the building.

The driver of the van turned the key, and the motor came to life. A simple movement of the gearshift on the column, and they were on their way. Within seconds, they were on the main road and heading for the rendezvous with Captain Frank. For the first few minutes, it was a quiet ride. Rob would glance at the driver of the van from time to time; he concluded that he couldn't be more than a year older than the boys who transferred their luggage.

Alicia was staring out the window she was seated next to. The countryside and the mountains were breathtaking, and the view was utterly amazing. Ronnie would smile at Alicia each time she would raise her hand to point at something and gently pat her knee. Shelley and Elaine were focused out the van's windows, trying to reason in their own minds if this was the right thing to do.

Shelley was the first to break the silence as she told the group they needed to stick together and always watch out for each other. Elaine was quick to chime in and agree with Shelley's statement. Then, she turned to Rob and said, "Rob, I just want you to know... I don't hold you responsible for what happened up here last year."

Ronnie and Shelley agreed openly with Elaine. Then, Shelley told Rob to make sure to always stay close to them, no matter what situation they encountered. Rob thanked everyone for their statements and turned to face the window. Only Shelley witnessed the tear that rolled off Rob's cheek.

The ride from the airport to the docking facility that held Captain Frank's boat was longer than the group remembered from last year. Alicia had no idea of the length of the journey and didn't mind the ride at all. She was too busy taking in all the sights and trying to contain the excitement of just being here. In her mind, this looked just like the kind of place for a so-called Hairy Man or Bigfoot. Almost the exact descriptions written in the books she had been reading and studying ever since Ronnie had returned home. Her enthusiasm worried Ronnie, though, as he felt she didn't fully understand the dangers of being here.

Just right before sunset, the young driver motioned straight ahead and said, "There it is, folks. Just a few more minutes, and we will be there."

Everyone scooted to the edge of their seats and took in the bay below them; several boats were moored to docks connected to the banks that sloped down to touch the water's edge. The view was majestic as they crossed the last small hill and began to weave down the road to the village. A few people were walking on the boats or the wooden planks that parallelled them. It seemed that each person's movement had a direct purpose or plan for what was going on at the time. The group realized that the only people who really didn't belong here was them.

As the young driver came to a stop and placed the van in park in front of an old wooden building, Rob suddenly realized that this was the command center from last year. The door at the top of the stairs swung open, and Captain Frank emerged. The best Rob could remember, it appeared that Frank had exactly the same attire on as the last time Rob had seen him. The same crusty ole hat, the same jacket, and it looked like the same old coffee mug in his hand. Probably had the same special sauce in it, too, and it didn't appear that ole Captain Frank had spent a lot of time trimming his beard either.

Once they were all out of the van, Captain Frank raised the mug and smiled. "Welcome back to our little corner of the world."

Rob raised his hand. "Thanks, Captain. How you been?"

Captain Frank said, "Oh, pretty good, Rob. How about you people step into my office? The young lad will take your luggage to the boat, and my men will store it for you guys. Got some grub for you people up here, and I'll explain our voyage while you are eating."

They all thanked the driver of the van, and as Rob passed by him, he held out a fifty-dollar bill. The young driver informed Rob that he had already been generously paid by the network. Rob smiled and told the young lad he didn't believe he would have a use for it where he was going, so the driver took the bill and quickly shoved it in his pocket.

They made their way up the stairs and into the building. Once inside, they discovered two fold-out tables with enough metal chairs surrounding them to accommodate everyone in the room. Right away, they all noticed the different variations of food laid on the tables as the captain shut the door. Captain Frank told everyone they weren't sure what to fix, so they kinda put a small buffet together. He looked at Rob, then told him that hopefully everyone could find something they liked.

All found a seat and began to dig in. It seemed that nothing was safe from the hungry travelers. Captain Frank finally took a seat at the head of the table and began to fill his plate. He glanced around the table at all the guests and soon figured out they had made the correct choices in preparing the food. The captain couldn't help but wonder why any of those from the port last year would want to return. He desperately wanted to ask but wasn't sure how or when to present the question. After several minutes, Rob leaned back in his chair, lifted his drink glass, and washed down the last bite of food. The captain lifted his coffee mug that contained the daily brew along with his special ingredient.

He couldn't stand it any longer, and the captain asked, "I'm just curious, Rob... Why did you and the others decide to come back?"

Everybody at the table looked at Rob, and after a short pause, he answered, "It's been a tough year for me, and I can't imagine what it's been like for these people, not to mention what the other families have gone through." Rob lifted his glass once again and took another sip, then lowered it and continued, "We all felt that the families of the others need closure, Captain Frank. We need to bring them home."

Captain Frank said, "The first party wasn't very talkative when we fed them. As a matter of fact, four of the gentlemen didn't speak at all, I don't believe."

Elaine interrupted, "That's part of the reason we are here, Captain. Rob is not sure of their motives."

Captain Frank turned from Elaine to Rob. "What motives? We were told this was purely a search and recovery mission...to find what we could and bring them home."

Rob replied, "That's what I was told by the network's vice president, but I overheard some conversations that led me to think otherwise."

"How so?" Frank asked.

Rob said, "Well, I think some or all of these so-called bodyguards want to kill one of these creatures. I think it's more of a hunting mission for them."

"Oh really?" Frank said. "Ever hear of anyone being successful at that?"

Rob answered, "No, I haven't, and I would like to keep it that way."

Captain Frank smiled. "I don't think you have anything to worry about, Rob. These things can take care of themselves."

Elaine said, "Captain, when I walked into the cabin of the boat last year as we were leaving the bay..."

Captain Frank smiled and said, "Yes?"

"Why did you smile and nod at me?" Elaine asked.

Captain Frank replied, "Not many people encounter the Hairy Man and survive, Elaine. Plus, I seen you make the gesture to the young one standing on the rock. I also watched it mimic your gesture, then it and the large one slipped back into the forest. Exactly what was that all about?"

Elaine took a sip of water and said, "The young one got injured in the cabin, and I discovered it in the back bedroom. For some reason that I'm not totally sure of, I administered first aid to the wound, and the mother gave me a stone. She held out her hand and looked me directly in the eyes. When I placed my hand out in front of me, she gently placed the rock into the palm of my hand."

Then, Elaine showed the captain the stone she wore on the chain around her neck. Shelley and Ronnie removed their rocks from the pouches to show Captain Frank as well.

Then, Shelley asked, "Did you know about the creatures?"

"Until Elaine communicated with the two standing on the rock, I had never actually seen one," the captain said. "Like everyone else, I've heard the stories about the port. My dad would tell me about the events that had taken place at the fish canary when I was a young boy, and he made me promise to never go ashore there. Of course, as young boys grow up, they have to press their luck, so two of my friends and I took a boat there one day to fish. As time passed on, we decided to hang around after dark just to see for ourselves if the creatures were indeed real. The sounds we heard coming from the forest that night convinced us that the promise I had made to my dad would not be broken. There were multiple grunts, howls, and tree knocks that pierced the cool night air as we sat anchored in the bay. We never left the boat, though. As a matter of fact, as soon as daylight broke, we fired up the boat and headed home."

Rob chimed in next, "At the airport, Conley said that some people warned the network about the port. Were you one of those people?"

Frank nodded yes. "Yeah... Me and some others told the guys from the network that going there might be a mistake. But after there were no issues with building the cabins, I think they just wrote it off as folklore of the area. I'm not really sure about going back this time either, Rob. Is it worth taking the chance?"

Rob gently shrugged his shoulders. "We all think so, especially for the creatures."

"My crew will help all they can, but I'm sure that none of them will go ashore," Frank said. "I know that I will not set foot on that soil—a promise is a promise."

Once again, Captain Frank lifted his coffee mug and took a drink, then he winked at Rob. Next, he showed the group to the building set up for all the team to sleep in. Once inside, the first members to arrive greeted Rob's group. Most of the earlier group had already settled on their cots to relax for the evening before turning in. Captain Frank told everyone that he would see them early in the morning and left the team to themselves.

For the next couple of hours, there was some small talk amongst the group. Rob and the others were quick to notice that the four bodyguards had little to offer in terms of conversation. Soon, everybody settled down for the night's rest, but sleep came hard for Ronnie. He couldn't help but think about Alicia's safety. Had it been a bad idea to let her tag along? Ronnie was questioning whether he even wanted to be here or not. What was waiting for them at Port Chatham?

Finally, he faded off to sleep, but the sleep he got was in small intervals between the many times his body would jerk, and he would abruptly awaken in the dimly lit room.

CHAPTER 5

R ob opened his eyes and immediately noticed that the darkness of the room had been replaced with a warm glow that illuminated everyone in their cots. All seemed to still be sleeping as he panned around the room, until he noticed the empty sleeping bag to his left. Rob slowly raised himself with his elbows and saw Elaine standing at the window, facing the harbor. She was staring motionless out the glass with her back to him.

Rob said, "Well, look at you. 'The early bird gets the worm' is what I've always heard. Not too sure if that's a prize to boast about, though."

Elaine turned and smiled. "Yes, I've heard that also. I guess it's just a habit that I have developed over the last year. I like to be the first at the office to get the day organized before the others arrive."

Rob unzipped his sleeping bag, sat up, and placed his feet on the floor. Even though Rob hadn't removed his socks from the night before, he could feel the chill of the concrete floor. He wondered just how the people of the area cope so well during the winter months. Rob could only imagine how cold the concrete floor would probably be in January or February, but these people were a lot tougher than him, and they fared just fine.

The silence was broken by a knock at the door, which opened into the makeshift sleeping area. Captain Frank appeared in the doorway. He told everybody to rise and shine; breakfast would be served in 30 minutes, and it would be wise not to miss it, for they wouldn't eat again until the boat was anchored at the port. The others began to moan and groan as they rustled to exit their sleeping bags. Captain Frank chuckled and told everyone he hoped they slept well in the comforts of the five-star hotel they had spent the night in. He then informed the team to roll up their sleeping bags. The crew would load the bags on the boat so that they could enjoy several more nights of sleeping in them there.

Elaine glanced back at Rob, and both of them smiled as the door closed. All put their boots on and rolled up the sleeping bags as Captain Frank had instructed. Soon, everyone was walking single file up the wooden steps to the same building where they had eaten the night before. Shelley took a quick look over the harbor and noticed the young boys were going to retrieve the sleeping bags to load onto the boat. She paused for a second and wondered about the decision to return here. As she turned back around, Shelley was met with raised eyebrows on Ronnie's face.

Ronnie said, "I guess it's too late to turn back now."

Shelley responded, "Yeah, I think so... Let's eat."

Once inside, everybody could smell the aroma of the bacon, pancakes, and the morning brew filling the air. As soon as they grabbed a seat, the servers began to place the morning's nourishment in front of them. Everybody picked up their utensils and heartily began to eat. The captain informed the group of the type of boat they would be taking to the port and what to expect once they were on the water. He looked at everyone with a hearty smile and informed them that the weather looked really good for the trip. The entire group seemed to nod in unison as they consumed the food. Next, Captain Frank asked if anyone needed a motion sickness patch in case the waves got a little rough. Whitney from the network and Aaron from the insurance company both raised their hands. The first mate handed each of them two small packets that contained a single patch each. After eating, both of them opened one of the patches and placed it on their necks behind the left ear. Rob smiled as they placed the empty packets on their plates.

Rob took a quick glance around the table as they finished their coffee, wondering if they were friend or foe. Maybe on the boat ride he could come to some conclusions on the group and what this was really all about, for now he was only sure about the captain and the returning members.

Twenty minutes later, the group was once again traversing the steps in single file on their way to the boat. Rob could see Captain Frank and the first mate waiting for them to board.

Captain Frank yelled and hoisted his hand high in the morning air. Next, he gestured for the team to come to the boat at the edge of the harbor. It was a short walk from the building to the pier on a path covered with small gravel and dirt. One could hear the small rocks crunching under boots as they took each step. The air was crisp and there was a small, gentle breeze blowing across the village. The bay was covered with tiny ripples that danced across the water. Once on the pier, there was a young boy that ushered everyone to the opened gate on the boat, and one at a time the guests boarded the boat. After all were safely aboard, the boy lifted the mooring ropes from the large wooden poles and tossed them onto the deck of the boat. One of the shipmates secured the ropes. As soon as the boat was free, Captain Frank began to pilot the ship away from the dock and out of the harbor. The newcomers went inside the ship, found a seat, and readied themselves for the journey. Rob, the ones returning, and Alicia all stayed on the deck, taking in the beauty of the area.

Finally, Alicia spoke, "This place is beautiful—just like you described it, Ronnie."

Ronnie smiled. "Don't let the scenery fool you. Where we are headed is even more majestic than this, but it's also a very dangerous place."

Elaine turned to Rob and asked, "Have you come to any conclusions about the others?"

Rob shook his head. "Not yet, but I'm pretty sure the bodyguards can't be trusted. The network and insurance people... I think they are probably looking for someone to hang last year's disaster on."

Shelley asked, "We plainly explained every detail... What more could they want?"

Rob leaned onto the ship's railing. "Nobody wants to admit that there is such a thing as this so-called Hairy Man," he said. "Most of the people at the network have made fun of the entire situation. They made light of me, all of you, and even my ex-wife didn't believe the stories. All I want to do is retrieve the ones who got left behind and somehow preserve the creatures along with their habitat."

Elaine asked, "And just how are we supposed to achieve that?"

Rob looked at the others. "Well, I'm not totally sure, but the captain has agreed to help us in a small way."

Ronnie asked, "In what way?"

Rob looked out over the water. "The boys who loaded our sleeping bags and gear onto the boat placed a weapon in each of our bags. Keep that information to yourselves."

Shelley looked up at an eagle soaring high above the bay. "Great. Now, we not only have to worry about the creatures, but also we have to second guess the people accompanying us."

Rob replied, "I'm sorry, guys, but I really think this is important."

Shelley patted Rob's shoulder. "I didn't mean anything by it, Rob. I think it's important, too, and we are all on your side."

Rob almost smiled. "Thanks, just don't take any chances out there."

As they turned to once again take in the view of the area, the sound of the side door opening caught everyone's attention. The individual stepped onto the deck of the boat and closed the door. Everyone could see it was Whitney from the network. She placed her hand on the railing and waved. The group returned the wave, and she slowly made her way to the group. For the most part, Whitney shuffled her feet on the wooden planks of the ship so as not to ever lose contact with them. As she approached the others, she felt her neck to assure herself that the patch was still in its rightful place.

"Guess you people can tell this is not exactly my cup of tea," Whitney said.

Everyone chuckled, and Elaine said, "It'll be okay. Try to just look out over the water and not down at it."

Whitney replied, "I'll take all the advice I can get; all of your help is appreciated."

Rob asked, "First time on a boat?"

Whitney answered, "Been on small boats on a lake, but never on the open sea."

"It's not too bad of a ride," Shelley said. "We won't get far from the land. You can always see the coastline and the mountains."

Whitney nodded. "That's good news... I think."

Everyone assured Whitney that the ride to Port Chatham would be uneventful, even though they knew that were circumstances that could arise and change all that. But for now, it was better to comfort Whitney than to throw a bunch of circumstances at her. Everyone watched the village slowly disappear as the boat drew closer to the mouth of the bay. Soon, they would be in the open sea.

Whitney was holding the railing of the boat with both hands. She only turned her head toward Rob to ask, "What do you know about these bodyguards?"

Rob answered, "Never seen them until the meeting in the conference room."

Whitney glanced back over the water. "You don't know them?"

Rob said, "No, I seen them in the building a day or two before the meeting, but I never met them until we all got together at the briefing. But... I never met you or Joe either until that day. As a matter of fact, I don't think I had ever seen you guys."

Whitney said, "No, I don't think we have ever crossed paths, but I've heard a lot about you."

"I can only imagine," Rob replied.

"Never heard anything bad, Rob. There's a lot of people who think highly of you."

Rob squinted his eyes just a little. "I'm sure there are those who don't."

"Maybe, but I've never heard anything. Mostly, people talk about what the events of last year have done to your life and career. I'm on your side, though. That's why I accepted this assignment, but I just don't think some of the people on this boat can be trusted."

Then, Rob asked, "What about Joe?"

Whitney glanced out and pointed to a bear walking the shoreline. After a short pause, she said, "Never met the man, Rob, never even heard of him."

The group glanced around at each other, but nobody held eye contact long enough for anyone inside the cabin to notice. As they turned to look out over the bay, there was a knock at the ship's window. The group turned to see Captain Frank smiling and motioning for them to come inside, so they moved to the door and entered the cabin. Captain Frank told them that the water outside the bay might be a little choppy, and he didn't want to have a man overboard. Whitney rolled her eyes and held onto Rob's arm as they made their way to a seat. Ronnie guided Alicia to a bench seat along the far side wall of the boat, and he sat down. Alicia placed her hand on Ronnie's shoulder and braced her knees against the bench. She continued to stare out the window, trying to take in every ounce of the scenery she possibly could.

The boat ride to Port Chatham was uneventful, something that Whitney was very thankful for. As the boat began to enter the mouth of the bay, Captain Frank heartily informed the group that they had arrived at their destination. The crew of the ship began to move around the boat like ants scurrying around the hill they call home. As the boat began to slow, Captain Frank told the team that it was now safe to stand on the deck and take in some fresh air if they so desired.

Alicia squeezed Ronnie's hand and smiled. She was the first to reach the cabin door and quickly turned the handle to open it. The sudden rush of the fresh outside air collided with Alicia's face, and she took a deep breath. She couldn't remember a time when she breathed air this clean. One by one, the team members slowly funneled through the door and evenly spaced themselves on the ship's deck on both sides. Everybody was scanning the crystal-clear waters and the mountains that surrounded the bay.

Whitney was the first to speak. She said, "This place is beautiful."

Shelley grinned but never took her eyes off the mountains. "That's exactly how we felt last year."

Elaine was scanning the shoreline, searching for the rock that the mother and juvenile creatures were standing on as they left the bay last year. "It's a beautiful place, but it has its secrets, Whitney. There's more here than meets the eye...and it already knows we are here."

Whitney looked around to see if any of the others were listening to the conversation, but because of the boat engine and the distance from the others she knew the conversation was private to them. "You really think they know?"

Elaine looked Whitney directly in the eyes. "I'm sure they knew as soon as we entered the bay. They are watching."

Ronnie spoke, "This is their home; we are the ones who don't belong here."

Then, Shelley pointed to the front of the boat. "There! Those long poles sticking out of the water—that was part of the old fish processing plant."

Whitney turned to look in the direction that Shelley had pointed and immediately noticed the eerie timbers protruding out of the water. There was a low fog that danced around the structure in front of them that was about two to three feet in height. The fog stretched from the old fish canary to the head of the bay. Everyone on the deck was now pointing or looking at the timbers sticking out of the water. As Elaine glanced back, she spotted the large rock at the water's edge that she had been searching for. She couldn't decide whether or not it was a good thing that nothing was standing on top of the boulder. Elaine remembered the feeling she experienced leaving the port as the young creature gestured to her. She lifted her stone from under her jacket and gripped it tightly.

Rob turned to Elaine and whispered, "You really think they already know we are here?"

Elaine answered, "Oh yeah... They know."

The engines of the boat slowed a little more, and they glided into a spot not too far from shore in front of the old processing plant. Then, Captain Frank reversed the engines to bring the vessel to a complete halt. Almost in the blink of an eye, the captain maneuvered the ship to a position that was perfectly parallel to the shoreline. Then, he ordered the anchors to be dropped, and the boat readied for their stay here at the port. Almost immediately, the boat came to life with young men scurrying around in all directions, preparing the ship for the stay. Their movements could be observed through the multiple small windows surrounding the deck as well as outside the cabin area.

Ronnie reached over and grabbed Alicia's hand. "See right up there? That's the two cabins from last year."

Shelley added, "It hasn't taken Mother Nature long to start reclaiming the area for her own again."

Ronnie responded, "Not very long at all. It's starting to grow up pretty quickly."

The sides and roofs of the cabins were still visible, but the thick underbrush and the small saplings surrounding the cabins had grown to the height of almost concealing the deck railings in some places. The native vines had already started to weave themselves through the spindles of the deck railings, and the steps were almost completely hidden from sight while standing on the ship's deck. The path from the shore could barely be seen as it made its way up the hill. The only spot still clear was the landing area for the rafts going ashore.

Elaine turned to Rob and asked, "Has anyone been here since we left?"

Rob answered, "To the best of my knowledge...no."

Suddenly, Captain Frank's voice pierced the late afternoon air: "Nobody's been here since our boat pulled out of the port last year, Elaine. If someone had ventured out here, I would know. Of course, there is the possibility that maybe some local boys might have visited the bay, but I'm certain nobody has gone ashore."

Rob asked, "How can you be so certain?"

Captain Frank grinned. "Been no reports of anybody going missing, Rob."

Everybody looked at Captain Frank, but not a single person returned the smile. Then, the captain ordered everyone to gather around close enough to hear what he had to say. He then informed them that the crew was situating the sleeping bags and their gear into two cabin rooms on the boat. Everyone's bunk would have their nametag on it, and their belongings would be stored underneath the bottom bunks. Captain Frank told the group that the evening meal was being prepared and should be ready in about an hour, and they should just relax and enjoy the view from the boat.

Captain Frank smiled, tipped his well-worn hat, and returned to the inside of the ship.

CHAPTER 6

As everyone began to observe all that was happening around them, Jeff Sizemore from the insurance company asked, "Rob, I know that everyone has been briefed about last year, but is there anything that you guys can add to help us out?"

Before Rob could even begin to answer, Elaine chimed in, "We gave the network, the authorities, and your people a very detailed description of all the events."

Joe Wilburn from the network spoke next, "Nobody is doubting a single word from the story that all of you conveyed. We just don't want any surprises."

Ronnie cleared his throat. "You hear all the birds chirping? That cheerful feeling you get from listening to the many outdoor sounds of nature here? The peace you're soaking in from not being involved in the hustle and bustle of back home? Well, that can change in the blink of an eye."

Shelley added, "When the forest goes silent, danger is in the air."

Harold, the smallest of the four men sent to protect the group, asked, "This so-called Hairy Man... Did any of you actually see it kill one of the others?"

Elaine said, "No, just the aftermath."

Aaron from the insurance company asked, "Then, how can we be sure it was one of them?"

Ronnie smirked and said, "Once again, just what are you trying to imply?"

"All I'm saying is maybe it could have been a bear, or possibly a mountain lion or something," Aaron said.

Elaine pointed her finger at Aaron. "Inside that cabin, I saw three of these creatures—a young one and two adults. They were not bears, mountain lions, or anything else that one would watch documentaries about on the television. These so-called Hairy Man creatures are real, and this place is their home. Believe me, we are the intruders here."

Rob spoke next, "I don't know of anything that was missed in our explanations of last year's events. We just need to go ashore and try to find the others so they can be returned to their families. However we decide to achieve this, we will have to figure it out. We need to remember to be careful at all times and pay close attention to our surroundings. Let's just do our job and leave the inhabitants of the port to live their lives the way they always have."

David Felder, a tall and rugged-looking man, asked, "Elaine, when you saw these things in the cabin... How big were they?"

Elaine glanced around. "The young one was probably between four and five feet tall. The one I considered to be the mother was maybe six to seven feet tall, and the one in the front room was at least eight or nine feet tall."

Wilson Wilkins, whose salt and pepper hair was partially hidden by his fedora hat, asked, "Nine feet? Are you sure, Elaine?"

Shelley, who was slightly slumped over on the ship's railing, said, "The one that was following Ronnie and I clearly had no problem picking us up like a sack of potatoes. Then, it carried us uphill to the abandoned road with ease."

Jeff Sizemore of the insurance company asked, "Shelley, why do you think the creature attacked the rest of your group, but not the two of you?"

Shelley shrugged her shoulders. "I'm not sure, Jeff, but the people who seemed to assist or help others didn't get attacked. Ronnie and I didn't leave Stan. Mark never left Andre. Willy went after Mark, and Elaine administered first aid to the young creature."

Whitney looked at Shelley. "So, you're saying that these creatures can show compassion?" she asked. "That they can reason?"

Ronnie answered Whitney, "The one that followed Shelley and I could have crushed us at any time, but for some reason it chose not to."

"When I got back to the crew's cabin, the door was completely knocked off the framework and was lying on the floor inside," Elaine said. "That took a lot of force to do."

Brad Easton placed his hands inside the pockets of his khaki shorts and looked at Elaine. He asked, "When you got back to the cabin, was anyone else there?"

Elaine lowered her head. "No... The others were there, but they were not alive."

Rob leaned against the outside of the ship. "All this information, every detail, is listed in the report that was handed to each of you."

Aaron spoke next, "I understand that, Rob, but sometimes it's just better to hear it from the horse's mouth. It makes it easier to get the full perspective of the situation."

Rob didn't care very much for Aaron's response; it sounded more like an interrogation than a genuine concern about the events of the previous year. He felt that the entire conversation on the boat deck was merely a test to see if everyone's responses still matched the details given in the report. So far, the only one that Rob remotely trusted was Whitney, but he wondered if she was possibly playing on both sides of the fence. Maybe he was trying too hard to analyze everybody here. Perhaps Whitney was completely genuine when she spoke to them at the beginning of the boat ride. All Rob knew for sure was that, right now, he only fully trusted the people from last year. In his mind, he wondered how he would feel this time next year.

The cabin door opened, and one of the young boat crew members smiled. "Soup's on, people. Let's eat."

One by one, they filed through the door as the young man held it open for them. Once inside, they were directed down a narrow corridor to a set of steps that led them down to the mess hall. The room was a lot smaller than the area they had eaten in that morning, but nobody seemed to mind since all were quite hungry from the ride to the port. Everyone took a seat at one of the two tables, which reminded Ronnie of a long picnic table, like the ones at the church shelter where his family attended when he was a young boy. Everybody was still segregated—the ones from last year at one table and the newcomers at the second table. Captain Frank immediately noticed that no friendships had been established between the members of the two groups.

The boat crew began to sit the evening's meal on the two tables in front of each person, and one by one they began to dig in. The food consisted of a hearty soup along with slices of homemade bread or crackers. For the most part, there was little conversation in the room. Only the occasional expression of gratitude to the chef and the crew was mentioned during the meal. Captain Frank watched the group closely as they ate and made several mental notes.

After finishing his meal, the captain asked, "Have you guys decided how to go about this mission?"

Rob answered, "We really haven't discussed it yet, but I have a map of the cabins and the surrounding area to get some ideas."

Brad Easton chimed in next, "That would be great to look at. I think we should divide into two groups, just like the crew and contestants did last year. That way, we can cover more ground and possibly accomplish our objective much faster."

"We could spread the map out on one of the tables to take a look at," Rob suggested. "The known locations are already marked on it."

Harold Birchfield said, "Sounds like a plan, Rob. If everyone is up for it, I say we get started."

Everybody nodded yes, and Rob left the room to retrieve the map from his gear. The crew quickly cleared the tables, and in a matter of minutes one couldn't tell that a meal had even taken place in the room. Rob returned with a large folder in his right hand. He took a position at the center of the table and removed the map. As he unfolded the large piece of paper, the others began to assemble around the table and focus on the map. Rob started to explain the markings on the map: first was the location of the two cabins and the old fish canary. Next was the old, abandoned road, the meadow at the head of the bay, and the homestead that had been discovered the year before. Then, Rob showed the location of Mr. Long up on the mountainside, which was highlighted in yellow. Next was the area of the meadow where Stan was found by his group, which was also highlighted in yellow.

Rob paused and stared at the map. Without saying a word, he simply ran his index finger down the paper to the location of the cabins. David Felder looked up from the table and said, "So, really, the only solid location we have to search is that of Mr. Long's."

Rob answered, "That's correct."

Ronnie interjected, "We only know where Shelley and I heard the gunshot from after our group separated. It seemed to come from the abandoned road at the point we started down to the meadow."

Aaron Nelson turned his head toward Elaine and asked, "And all you recovered from Dave was his arm, right, Elaine?"

"Yes, it was lying on the deck of the contestants' cabin," Elaine said. "The far side of the cabin."

David glanced around the entire group. "Then, we'll have to search around the cabin. It would only make sense that he's there somewhere."

Wilson Wilkins tilted his fedora hat up to expose his forehead and said, "I agree with the two-group approach. We could split the four of us, and there would be two bodyguards for each search party. We could place one network and one insurance representative in each group also. I think Ronnie and Shelley would be most helpful at the meadow. Rob and Elaine could go with the group to the mountainside. We can all stay in contact with each other and the boat."

"I think that sounds pretty good if everyone is in agreement," Rob said.

Everybody looked around at each other and nodded. Rob folded up the map and placed it back into the folder. Captain Frank informed the group that right after breakfast some of the crew members would shuttle them to the shore. Next, he informed the group that the ship's crew would return to the boat and wait for instruction. If anyone needed assistance, they were to shout back with the walkie-talkie, and the crew would return to the shore to pick them up.

Everyone nodded yes, and Brad Easton asked, "Anybody other than the ones from last year got a preference to which group they are in?"

Whitney was the first to respond, "I'll go with Rob and Elaine's group."

Aaron Nelson raised his hand. "Doesn't matter to me."

"Then, how about you join Rob's group?" Wilson asked.

"You got it," Aaron agreed.

Wilson said, "Harold and I will round out the group. That makes the rest of you in the second party... Everybody good with that?"

All the members of the search parties agreed with the placements of the teams. They nodded their heads and verbally agreed with the grouping assignments. The bodyguards returned to their sleeping quarters to ready their equipment and weapons for the first day ashore, and the representatives of the network and insurance companies gathered at the end of the table. Everyone remaining in the mess hall was given a cup of coffee by a couple of the young boys, and the returning group ventured back out onto the deck of the ship. The air had become quite crisp while the people were inside, and the sun was beginning to fade fast. Only about half of its orange glow was visible across the top of the mountains, and the shoreline had begun to grow dark.

As everyone gathered at the front of the boat, Alicia asked, "Ronnie, do I get to go ashore with you and Shelley?"

Ronnie sighed, "I knew you were gonna ask... I really wish you would stay on the boat."

Alicia smiled. "You know I want to go."

"I don't know, Alicia. I'm afraid of what could happen out there."

Alicia slightly tilted her head and winked. "The bodyguards have weapons, and so do we. As long as we are not caught out there after dark, it'll be okay."

Rob laughed and said, "Don't think you're gonna win this one, Ronnie."

Ronnie smiled, "I can't remember ever winning one. Why should now be any different?"

Everybody laughed and Ronnie turned to Alicia. "Okay, you win. Just make sure you stay close to me and Shelley. Never leave our side."

Alicia grinned from ear to ear. "You got it, boss."

Ronnie replied, "Yeah, boss... Right."

Just then, the cabin door opened, and once again Whitney emerged. She spotted the others and began to move toward them, gently sliding her hand along the railing. The others couldn't help but smile as she traversed the deck. Whitney seemed to be adjusting to boat life somewhat, even though she still shuffled her feet as she moved.

Once she reached the group, she let out a small sigh. "It's amazing what the air smells like here; no pollution or man-made odors."

Rob smiled. "Nothing but fresh air. A person could get used to this."

Elaine was intently watching the shoreline as the group's conversation continued about the great outdoors. Suddenly, she saw movement, just to the left of the trail that led from the shore to the cabins. The lighting at the edge of the tree line had grown dim, and there were shadows everywhere, but she continued staring at the spot hoping to get another glimpse of whatever it was she had seen. Next, there was a large splash that disturbed the calm water between two of the remaining support poles of the old canary facility. All turned in the direction of the splash.

Whitney asked, "Was that a fish?"

Even though the others had a different explanation, Ronnie replied, "Sounded like a big one."

Whitney turned back to the others and said, "Sure did. I researched the fishing village, and it sounds like it was really doing well. That is, right up until the workers all left."

"According to all accounts, it was a booming business," Rob said.

Whitney wrapped her arms around her chest. "Yes, it was... Well, I've had about all this chilly air I can stand. I'm going back inside to get warm. See you guys in a bit."

"We'll be there as soon as we finish our coffee."

As soon as the door to the cabin shut, Ronnie turned to Rob and said, "I don't think that was a fish."

"That was something thrown into the water, and it was pretty good size too," Shelley added.

Way up on the mountain, there were three distinctive knocks that sounded like two baseball bats hitting together, then off the bow down the shoreline came three more knocks. There was a moment of silence. Then, from beyond the meadow high on the mountainside came the bellowing howl that echoed across the bay. It wasn't something that could be heard from inside the ship, but from the deck, there was no mistaking what the sound was.

Shelley continued to stare in the direction of the meadow. "That's the same sound we heard at the meadow the last time, and there was more than one creature making the noise."

Ronnie said, "There's several creatures that call this place home. Those wood knocks are part of their communication practices."

"According to all the books I've read, they communicate in several methods. Some even say they have their own language," Alicia said.

"Their own language?" Rob asked.

"Not necessarily like ours, but series of grunts and noises they make with their mouths."

Suddenly, there was another splash in the front of the boat halfway between it and the shore. The ripples made by the object were just barely visible in the water as they raced toward the boat. The forest had almost become black in the darkness that had overtaken the bay, and as quickly as the events had started, they ended. Silence filled the air, and all became calm. Only the lonely call of the owl on the hill behind the cabins pierced the darkness.

Elaine whispered, "They know we are here."

After about five more minutes, the group made their way to the cabin door and entered the ship. Once inside, they heard talking and laughter coming from the mess hall. They joined the others and took a seat at the tables. The crew were telling stories about themselves and growing up in the area. Nobody mentioned anything about the events that had just taken place outside; they merely joined in as spectators listening and laughing at the young men's adventures.

The stories continued as the evening wore on, and everyone seemed to enjoy the break from the task at hand. At about 10:30, Elaine began to yawn and informed the group that she was going to call it a night. Everyone concluded that it was a good idea for all to get some rest, for tomorrow would be a busy day. Captain Frank wished everyone sweet dreams and told them he would personally provide their wake-up call in the morning.

One of the young men of the boat crew told everyone to leave their coffee cups on the table and he would take care of them. They all thanked him, and Ronnie patted the young man's shoulder and said, "We're all going to owe you guys a big night on the town with a big meal."

The young man laughed, "Big night on the town? You must have had your eyes closed back at the village when you people were there."

Everyone laughed and retired to their respective rooms. Whitney was the only newcomer in the room of the returning group. Rob figured Captain Frank had observed her talking to them on the ship's deck and decided to place Whitney in their room. Out of all the others, Rob was happy that it worked out this way. Soon, everyone was asleep in their bunks, but for some it was not a restful night.

Ronnie tossed and turned repeatedly. Elaine wondered if the boat was still being watched.

CHAPTER 7

Early the next morning, Captain Frank opened the newcomers' door. "Rise and shine, people," he called out.

He repeated the gesture at the second door, only this time he added that the early bird gets the worm. Then, Captain Frank heartily laughed and shook his head. Everyone rolled out of their bunks and began preparing for the day's adventure. After taking the last step of putting on their hiking boots, they all made the trip to the mess hall.

As soon as everyone entered the room, the smell of bacon and fresh coffee was the first thing to greet them. Next came the aroma of fried eggs and toast. They all sat in the same exact positions as the night before, almost like they were assigned to a particular seat. Captain Frank observed the group as they took their seats and concluded they were just creatures of habit, or perhaps everybody was still half asleep and hadn't realized they sat down in the same location as the night before. Either way, he just smiled again and shook his head. After the group was seated and began to eat, the captain removed the flask of special sauce to add to the old mug he gripped in his hand. Rob was the only one to see the captain juice up his coffee. He merely grinned and raised his coffee cup to toast Captain Frank. The captain produced a wide smile, then returned the gesture to Rob. Knowing quite well they had a busy day ahead of them and there probably wouldn't be a break for lunch, everybody ate until their bellies were full—some maybe a little too full. All the members of the search party savored the morning coffee to the last drop and departed the mess hall to finalize the preparations to go ashore.

In the returning group's cabin room, Whitney was the first to put on her small backpack and leave the room. She had only slightly participated in the small talk of the others during the preparations. The rest of the other group waited until the door had been securely closed before removing the pistols that Captain Frank's crew had conveniently supplied for them. Ronnie and Rob clipped the holsters on the inside of their belts to conceal them. The women all placed their pistols in a zippered compartment of their backpacks, and everyone took a quick glance at each other after securing the weapons.

Alicia looked at Ronnie and said, "I feel safer with these things... I just hope a need for them doesn't arise."

Ronnie replied, "Yeah, me too."

Rob said, "I'm still not sure about Whitney; time will tell whose side she is really on. Just be careful what you say to her."

"I think it's better if we keep the weapons our little secret for now," Shelly added.

Elaine said, "I agree. Everybody, keep a sharp eye out when we get close to the shore and pay attention for any odd smells. Our advantage is that we have been here before, except for Alicia, but hopefully if there is danger, we will be quick to recognize it."

Rob looked at Elaine. "You three have the experience, so you guys will have to guide Alicia and I."

Ronnie pointed at Rob and Alicia and said, "We need to stay together. Don't wander off; the two of you must remain close."

"Don't worry," Rob said. "I'm staying close to one of you at all times... My heart is already about to pound out of my chest."

"Just don't get too focused on searching without watching the surroundings... Okay?" Shelley said.

Rob nodded. "Deal."

The cabin door swung open, and Captain Frank leaned in. "Ready, people? My crew are waiting at the rafts."

Everybody nodded yes, and they followed the captain down the corridor and outside to the aft section of the ship. Once there, the group were met with a set of steps leading down to a small platform, from which they would board the rafts. The first group were just leaving the loading zone, and the young crew revved the engine while maneuvering the vessel for the shoreline. One by one, they slowly moved down the steps to the landing area where another young man assisted them in boarding the raft. The captain took ahold of Rob's arm, and with a stern look on his face told him to pay attention at all times.

Rob was last to board the raft, and a third young man on the landing platform pushed the raft away from the boat. The driver twisted the throttle to provide power, and the raft was on its way to the shore. For some unknown reason, Rob noticed that the water of the bay was as smooth as a sheet of glass and there was not a cloud in the sky. Suddenly, he caught sight of an eagle coming down the tree line in a perfect gliding pattern. Just as Rob pointed at it for everybody to see, the eagle folded its wings and entered into a steep dive. It swooped between two of the old processing plant support poles and extended its claws toward the surface of the water. In the blink of an eye, it picked a fish out of the water and began to flap its wings to carry the morning's meal to a safe place to enjoy it.

The driver of the raft placed his hand on Rob's shoulder and said, "Now that's how you catch a fish."

Rob smiled and nodded yes. In less than a minute, the driver of the raft reduced the throttle on the outboard engine and the raft began to slow. The crew of the raft for the first landing party backed away from the shoreline and turned the vessel to give the second raft clearance to slide onto the sandy landing area. The first group were milling around on both sides of the landing spot when the second raft slid into position. Some were cautiously looking along the shoreline, while others were staring intently up the hillside to the cabins. A young man in the front of the raft jumped onto the shore, one foot landing dryly in the soft dirt and the other splashing in the water of the bay. One by one, he assisted the riders of the raft onto the shore. Just before he pushed the raft back into the bay, he reminded the group to call on the radio if they needed assistance. This time, both of the young man's feet impacted the water just seconds before he leaped onto the raft. He teetered briefly on his belly and rotated his body, swinging his legs into the front of the raft. The driver switched the engine to reverse and slightly revved the engine. Soon, they maneuvered the vessel in the same manner as the first crew and sped back toward the ship lying anchored in the bay.

Brad Easton was the first to address the group: "Okay, people, let's all stay alert. I'll go first up the trail and Wilson will bring up the rear."

Next was Harold Birchfield. He said, "David and I will space ourselves amongst the group so that everyone is covered by the bodyguards. Let's go nice and easy."

The bodyguards readied their weapons, and the group filed in according to the manner they had been instructed. As they methodically moved up the trail, Rob couldn't help but think the bodyguards appeared like soldiers searching out any enemy that lay in their path. He wasn't quite sure at the moment if this was a good thing or not, but it almost provided him with a little assurance of security even though Rob already didn't like these men.

To Elaine, it seemed that they were moving really slowly as they traversed the path. She couldn't believe how much it had grown since last year. Mother Nature was quickly reclaiming the area; at spots you could barely see any dirt for the vines running across it. The scrub bushes had begun to reach toward each other from the two sides of the trail to the point that the sound they made scraping on each person's pants could clearly be heard all around. Elaine thought to herself, *So much for sneaking back to the cabins.*

Shelley continuously tested the air for any strange odors. Even though a year had gone by, she knew there would be no doubt in her mind if she smelled one of the creatures. Ronnie was walking behind Alicia, making sure she didn't have any trouble going up the path. He was still wondering why he let her come in the first place. Ronnie was questioning in his mind why either of them were there. Maybe they could just find the others and get out of this place without incident.

The group finally reached the top of the trail, and the path split into two trails. One path led to the old, abandoned road, and the other to the cabins. Elaine felt a rush of emotions run through her, and she put her right hand on her chest. She slid her hand inside the light, unzipped jacket she had on and squeezed the stone through her shirt.

Everybody came to a stop where the trail divided, and after a few seconds of scouring the area, Brad turned to face the group. "Everybody okay so far?"

The group acknowledged Brad with a quick nod—all but Wilson, who had an attentive eye on the group's back.

Brad said, "Let's take a look at the cabins."

Slowly in single file, the group made their way down to the crew cabin, and everyone stood in the area in front of the steps until Brad reached the deck and took a quick look around the outer portion of the cabin. Brad motioned for the rest of the group to come up on the deck as he scanned the bushes and the second cabin. One at a time, they climbed the steps until everyone was finally on the deck at the front of the cabin.

The first thing that struck Elaine's eyes was the dingy, dark stains on the deck planks at the front door. She stood there wondering what exactly Sasha went through in those final moments. In her mind, she was hoping that Sasha was not conscious in the final minutes of her life. Elaine remembered the fear she felt while hiding on the deck of the other cabin, but there was no way it compared to this.

Brad Easton gave Elaine a few more seconds, and then he asked, "Elaine, was that where Sasha was attacked?"

Elaine slowly raised her head. "I'm pretty sure it is; she was lying in the bushes down by the bottom of the steps."

"And Tim, he was inside, right?" Brad said.

Elaine answered, "Yes."

"What about Betty?"

Elaine slightly tilted her head. "I don't know about Betty. The people that came to get us didn't see her. But nobody spent a lot of time searching for Betty or Dave. They just wanted to get us out of here."

Brad asked, "But both of them were here at the cabins?"

Elaine looked over to the contestant cabin and nodded. "Yes, Dave was over at that cabin, and when I left to check on him Betty was still in this cabin."

Brad said, "I think that both of them must be close by. Let's go inside and look around."

Brad entered the crew cabin first through the broken door, and after his eyes adjusted to the light, he began to survey the inside of the cabin. There was nothing that seemed to be out of place from the description the survivors gave in their account of what had taken place. It didn't appear that anyone or anything had been inside since the rescue. For a few minutes, there was complete silence until the bodyguards began to search the place.

Harold Birchfield pointed to the window facing the other cabin. "Was this window broken when you guys were rescued?"

All the survivors stared at the window and then at each other. Finally, Elaine said, "I'm not sure. I don't ever remember looking at it."

The representatives of the network and insurance company hadn't spoken a word since getting off the rafts. Now they gathered in front of the fireplace, observing the activity of all the others and listening to every word of the conversation. They watched closely as the men moved throughout the cabin, stopping periodically to take what appeared to be careful observations of the cabin's interior.

Harold broke the silence this time with, "There's a bullet hole in the trim around this window, and there's glass on the inside floor as well as outside on the deck."

David Felder said, "That means that the window may have been broken in both directions."

"Maybe something busted the window reaching in and then broke more of the glass as it retracted its arm," Harold said.

"Maybe more went out that window than just an arm."

Rob interrupted, "You think something pulled Betty through that window?"

Elaine gasped, "Betty had been watching out the window to see if she could spot Dave. I saw her watching me as I moved around in my search at the other cabin."

Harold glanced back at the broken glass. "That kind of makes sense. When whatever happened at this window, Tim probably fired a shot in this direction."

Wilson was still standing guard at the door watching the group's back. He raised his head and studied the area above the door opening. "Looks like another hole above the door facing."

Brad was standing at the end of the kitchen counter. "And this is where Tim was lying, between the counter and the table?"

Elaine answered, "Yes."

Brad looked over to David. "So, as things were happening, Tim was trying to react and fire the weapon."

David said, "Sure seems that way. It must have been happening so fast that he didn't have time to take good aim."

Harold said, "No, he was just shooting in the direction of the events."

Ronnie and Alicia were standing on the opposite side of the cabin from the broken window, and Ronnie pointed to the wall beside that window. "Brad, this looks like another bullet hole in the wall beside the window."

Brad responded, "Maybe Tim saw something move past that window, too; there's also a hole in the floor where Tim was found."

Then, Brad peered through the door to the bedroom. "Elaine... Back here is where you discovered the young, injured creature?"

Elaine said, "Yes, it was squatting down next to one of the bunks."

"Come and show me," Brad said.

Brad and Elaine walked into the bedroom, and she pointed to the area where she found the juvenile creature. "He was right there."

Brad asked, "Was the bedroom window broken when you came in here?"

Elaine looked at the window. "I couldn't say for sure; I was scared to death and for some reason I only focused on the small one."

"So, it was smaller than the other ones?" Brad asked.

Elaine paused for just a second, "Yeah, the one I figured to be the mother was big, but the creature standing in the front room was massive, Brad."

Brad positioned himself in the room where he could see the spot that Tim was found. Then, he turned to face the back wall of the room. Brad pointed to a spot just about four feet off the floor and said, "There's another hole. Tim must have fired a shot at the young creature, but by this time he probably was already in a panic. He most likely didn't even know what he had shot at. Tim either grazed the juvenile, or it cut itself coming through the window."

Elaine turned to look at the broken window and then to the hole in the wall. "Can't really blame Tim for his actions."

Brad said, "No, but I'm assuming that while he was focused on the bedroom, something entered through the door and attacked him. Maybe his last shot was the one into the floor while it had ahold of him, but I'm kinda guessing on that one. Come on, let's get back to the others."

Once Brad and Elaine got to the front room of the cabin, he explained what they had found in the bedroom, and after several minutes of discussion everybody came to the same conclusion of how the events of that fateful night unfolded. The entire group exited the cabin and moved to the deck beside the first broken window they had discovered. There they found similar stains not only on the deck but also on the exterior wall of the cabin. After some reasoning, they realized that Betty's body had probably impacted the side of the cabin several times. They hoped she was nearby, and it would be possible to locate her to take the remains home.

Next, the group made their way to the contestant cabin and searched it. The cabin appeared much the same as the first one. It also didn't look like anyone or anything had been inside it, nothing other than some small rodents. Then, Elaine showed the others where she had found David's arm. Once again, the same discolored stains were on the deck, and a few were on the cabin wall.

The bodyguards scanned the surrounding area around the cabins from the safety of the deck. Finally, Brad said, "I think we need to go back to the boat and come up with a search plan for the area around the cabins. We'll eat a good, hot meal and start fresh in the morning. Does that sound good to everyone?"

They all agreed and radioed the boat for the rafts. The small hike from the cabins to the shore was totally uneventful. There were no musky odors and no strange noises, and soon all 13 people were safely back on the boat.

CHAPTER 8

Each group returned to their respected cabin quarters to unload and put away their gear. Rob was the last one in line coming in when he noticed Captain Frank looking at him. The captain simply nodded for Rob to come over, and once everybody had started down the corridor he leaned against one of the inside walls and looked Rob straight in the eye. "Kinda a short day out there," Frank said. "Everything okay?"

Rob whispered, "Yeah, we went through the cabins. Doesn't appear that anything has been in either one."

Captain Frank raised his eyebrows. "No luck in finding the others there?"

Rob shook his head. "No...but nobody ventured down into the brush surrounding the cabins. Seemed like they were only trying to verify Elaine's story and come up with some conclusions on how to search for the others."

Captain Frank asked, "What about the network and insurance people?"

Rob shook his head again. "Can't figure them out, Captain. They didn't ask or offer anything the entire time we were out there."

Captain Frank said, "Keep an eye on those four, Rob... They may just be trying to hang this on the survivors."

Rob smiled. "I will. Supposedly we are going to formulate a plan to begin searching first thing tomorrow."

Captain Frank nodded, and Rob exited the room. Rob made his way to the quarters of his party. Just as he reached for the knob, the door swung open, and Whitney emerged from the room. She and Rob exchanged smiles as he stepped aside so she could maneuver down the small corridor. After watching Whitney enter the other cabin quarters for the rest of the people, Rob stepped into the cabin room. He closed the door behind him and looked around the room; everyone else was watching him.

Shelley was the first to speak. "What was that all about up at the cabins?"

Rob answered, "Not totally sure, people. Maybe they are still trying to assess the situation."

Elaine said, "They seem to be trying to confirm my story."

Rob responded, "Yeah, kinda seemed that way to me, too."

Ronnie was sitting on his bunk, and he turned his head toward Rob. "How come the other four didn't contribute in any manner while we were up there?"

Rob removed his backpack and sat down on his bunk. "I'm not sure about that either, but I think the bodyguards want a clear picture of what we need to do as a group when we search. We decided to split into two groups to search the area away from the cabins, but maybe they want us to stick together at the cabins. I think they are trying to feel this out as they go. We'll know for sure when we all sit down together."

Elaine slapped her hands on her knees. "Brad did say we needed to come up with a plan to search around the cabins. Possibly we are being a little paranoid about the rest of the group...but I still don't trust them. I'm just not sure who can and cannot be trusted. It's tough thinking about these creatures and the other members of the search party all at the same time."

"Let's just watch out for each other, but keep an open mind about the others," Rob said.

Suddenly, there was a knock at the door, and Rob rose from his bunk and approached the door. He turned the knob and opened the door; Whitney once again smiled at Rob and informed him the others were ready to discuss tomorrow's search plans. Rob told Whitney they were ready and asked Shelley to get the map of the area so they could try to pinpoint some spots for the search. Shelley grabbed the folded piece of paper, and everybody exited the room and walked single file down the corridor to the mess hall. As Rob and the second group entered the room, the other members had already secured a cup of coffee and taken a seat at one of the tables.

David Felder stood and said, "Great, you guys brought the map. Maybe we can figure out exactly where to search for Dave and Betty."

Shelley handed the paper to Rob, who unfolded it and laid it upon the table. Shelley grabbed two cups of coffee—one for her and one for Rob.

Elaine leaned over the table, looking at the map. "Where do we need to look first?"

Wilson was quick to answer, "Considering where you found the arm, I think Dave may be down the hill off that side of the cabin...toward the bay."

Harold looked at Elaine. "It would only make sense that the creature would have tossed him downhill."

Wilson added, "It's possible that it may have thrown him towards the back of the cabin, but either way he should be on that side."

Joe Wilburn from the network asked, "Exactly what are we going to be looking for? I mean... After this amount of time, what condition are the bodies going to be in?"

Harold answered, "There may be clothing fragments that we'll find, but as far as the victims are concerned, I would think we are only looking for bones."

Jeff Sizemore from the insurance company said, "You think they have already decomposed down to just skeletons?"

"This is a harsh environment, and unfortunately there are a lot of scavengers up here in the wild," David said.

Just then, Captain Frank entered the room to say, "The man is probably correct; very little is wasted up here. It's important to find them now, because this time next year there may not be any bones left."

Elaine was next to ask, "But there were bones in the old homestead from over 75 years ago?"

Captain Frank said, "Yes, Elaine, but they were protected from the elements, and most of the things that like to gnaw on bones don't live in houses."

Elaine said, "Yeah, I reckon so."

"So, we need to search this area right here," Brad said.

Elaine glanced at the area that Brad was circling on the map with his index finger. "Yes, I'd say that's our best chance of finding Dave."

Aaron Nelson from the insurance company asked, "What about Betty, where do we look for her at?"

Harold spoke again, "Once again, the creature more than likely threw her down the hill, so we should search below the cabin first."

Brad agreed with Harold. "I think Harold is right; it's as good a place to start as any."

Shelley asked, "Do we search around the cabins as one big group or split up?"

Brad said, "Let's do the cabins as a single group, and once we find Dave and Betty, we'll split up to search for the others."

Everyone agreed with the plan for the next morning and sat around finishing their coffee. The boat's crew informed them that the next meal would be ready shortly and they were welcome to stay at the tables or wander around the boat. Everybody thanked the young boys and headed for the deck to take in some fresh air.

Once outside of the boat, the group all congregated at the bow and began to take in the beauty of the wilderness they were all visitors of. There was still quite a bit of daylight left, and they could take in the activity of the bay. A mother whale and her calf were periodically breaching the surface of the water toward the mouth of the bay. An eagle was gliding down the shoreline looking for an easy meal to swoop down on and grab. There were small birds chirping while darting from limb to limb on the trees that bordered the bay's water. Up the bay, a mother bear and her two cubs were aimlessly wandering in the soft sediment of the bank heading for the meadow at the head of the bay.

Alicia finally broke the silence, "This place is utterly amazing. Wonder what it would have looked like if the people of the fishing village could have stayed?"

Ronnie turned to Alicia and said, "Honey, we were all starstruck by the wonder of this place a year ago, but believe me... It can turn into something pretty violent in the blink of an eye."

Shelley added, "Absolutely, Alicia, things can change fast."

Harold Birchfield, the smallest of the bodyguards, asked, "I know we've talked a lot about the cabins and the activity around them, but would it be possible to discuss the meadow and the homestead a little?"

Shelley responded first, "None of us actually went to the homestead. All we know about it is Mark and Willy's description. And neither of them were interested in returning to this place, but Ronnie and I were at the meadow."

Harold said, "We, being the ones who were not here last year, have all read the reports from a year ago. I would like to say that I have no doubt about the accuracy of each account of the events. There's just more to hearing it directly from the horse's mouth rather than reading it on a sheet of paper."

Ronnie slowly leaned onto the railing of the ship and looked toward the shoreline. "We all looked toward the mountain to the left of the meadow as soon as the creature howled. It couldn't have been more than a couple of seconds until Bill turned to look at each of us in our various spots in the meadow, and Stan was gone." Ronnie rose from the railing but continued to stare at the shoreline. "It happened so fast. I mean...one second we were searching for clues, and the next second Stan was dead."

David Felder, the rugged-looking bodyguard, said, "Ronnie, you and

Shelley said that you heard a gunshot near the old, abandoned road?"

Ronnie replied, "Yes, sir."

"Wonder if Bill may have actually hit one of these creatures?"

"We have no idea," Ronnie said.

"There were no strange noises coming from that direction after the gunshot?" David asked.

"No, to tell the truth, I was so fearful I can't even remember hearing anything. It seems like there were more vocalizations after the shot was fired, but they didn't sound like an injured animal."

David glanced at Shelley and then turned back to Ronnie. "When did you guys realize that something was following you?"

Ronnie answered, "As we were working our way down the shoreline, almost immediately as the trees began to border the water."

"It wasn't exactly following us," Shelley interjected. "It would walk almost even with us as we moved down the shoreline."

"Why do you think the creature did that?" asked David.

Shelley shook her head. "I don't know... I even asked Ronnie several times about the creature and its intentions."

Two of the other bodyguards, Brad and Harold, were watching the facial expressions of Ronnie and Shelley as they answered David's questions. Wilson Wilkins was intently looking toward the cabins and scanning their surroundings. He seemed oblivious to anything that was being said on the ship's deck.

Rob took mental notes of everything that was happening, trying to figure out in his own mind what exactly was going on. Rob studied Wilson's actions more than anyone else. Why was he not paying attention to the conversation? Why was he not asking any questions?

David turned to Shelley. "When you and Ronnie collapsed going up the game trail, why do you think the creature acted the way it did?"

"You mean picking us up and carrying us up to the old road?" Shelley said.

David asked, "Yes, any ideas on that?"

Shelley said, "When I felt the creature pick me up... I really thought it had made the move we had been waiting on all night. At some point, either from exhaustion or fear, I lost consciousness. I don't remember anything until Ronnie shook my shoulder and I awoke in the crude shelter."

Jeff Sizemore interjected, "It doesn't make any sense. It had already killed Stan...probably Bill and Sandy too. Why did it carry the two of you and Stan to the road, then build a shelter to protect the three of you?"

Ronnie snapped back, "We explained all this in the reports. We really don't know the *why* of the things that took place. Maybe Elaine is right; it spared all of us simply because we tried to help others. Not being rude, but the creatures didn't exactly set us down and explain what was going on in their heads."

Jeff slowly raised his hands out in front of his chest. "I didn't mean it that way, Ronnie. We are just trying to get a feel of the situation."

Ronnie tilted his head. "Sorry, it just seems like we are being interrogated. I can assure you people that we divulged everything we know in our reports."

Brad Easton was the next to speak, "Ronnie, we are all new to this place and its surroundings. I guess we just don't want any surprises while we are doing our job. You guys endured everything that happened here, and that's the best playbook there is to study. We apologize for continuing to prod you survivors with questions, but I think the answers may help us out there."

Elaine pointed in the direction of the cabins. "Listen, people, this area is not just some hocus-pocus place where we can't explain what we saw. These creatures are real. I've seen them, and I believe the inhabitants of the fishing village witnessed them too. The drawings and the stories those people left behind over 75 years ago are real. Even I was pretty skeptical when we arrived last year. But now, there's not a doubt in my mind that this creature exists, and I'm sure that the people of the fish canary felt the same way."

Just as Elaine finished speaking, one of the deckhands opened the door and informed the group that dinner was served. Everyone slowly made their way along the side of the boat and entered the ship.

Elaine was the last one in line, and she continued to stare at the landing zone while she slid her hand down the railing of the ship. She had been staring at a particular spot the entire time she was speaking. Just a few feet to the left of the sandy shore in the thick brush was a dark spot that had caught her eye; the spot hadn't moved while she was speaking. Elaine broke eye contact with the shore as she turned to enter the ship. Before closing the door, she took another look at the shore, and the dark spot was gone.

CHAPTER 9

Everyone sat at the picnic-style tables and heartily enjoyed the meal that had been prepared by the crew for them. There was mostly just small talk shared by the people of the room. For the most part, the bodyguards and the insurance and network representatives conversed among themselves, while the others tried to catch up on each other's lives for the last year. Periodically, one of the young deckhands would enter the dining area to assist with refills, but they never interjected themselves into the conversation. They only smiled and nodded at the group as they were thanked for the service.

Captain Frank entered the room and slowly made his way to the coffee pot that was situated in the corner of the mess hall. After filling his coffee mug companion that he always seemed to carry with him, one of the crew emerged from the kitchen with the captain's plate. He graciously smiled at the young man and thanked him, then Captain Frank added the special flavoring to the cup and returned the flask to his coat pocket.

Just as the captain turned to grab a seat, he was met with Rob's approach, and Rob whispered, "I'll be glad to up your salary a little if you could possibly share a little of that special sauce."

Both men grinned, and the captain retrieved the flask once again. "I would be more than happy to share, Rob, but let's keep it a secret. We don't want to have to supply the entire group with the ole special sauce. We might just run out before the mission is accomplished."

Both men nodded, and after pouring a little in Rob's cup, the captain returned the flask once again to the security of his coat pocket, picked up his plate and mug, and continued to the table. Rob slowly took a sip of the cup and immediately turned toward the wall. He tried to hide the cough with his hand as he covered his mouth, but Captain Frank was watching intently. When Rob turned to face the others, he noticed the big grin on the captain's face. He merely smiled and shook his head as Rob headed for the deck of the boat. As he passed by the captain, Rob patted Captain Frank on the shoulder. The captain's entire body shook when he chuckled as Rob walked by. Rob exited to the outside of the ship and made his way to the bow.

For the entire meal, every time Elaine looked at the other table she noticed that Whitney from the network had been staring at one or more of her group. Every now and then, she caught Whitney looking in her direction. Each time she did, Whitney would only return a smile in her direction and glance away. Elaine desperately wanted to know what was going on in her mind. Elaine was the next to finish and told the others she was going to join Rob for some fresh air. The rest of the group said they would be out shortly.

Elaine closed the door and began to search the ship's deck for Rob. It only took a couple of seconds to spot him on the bow. Elaine slid her hand along the ship's railing as she approached Rob. The chill in the air had already started filling the evening at the bay as the sun began to set behind the mountains that bordered the bay. Elaine pulled the jacket she wore up around her neck. Then, she grabbed Rob's coffee cup and took a big sip before he could stop her. By the immediate gasp and cough from Elaine, Rob knew it was too late.

Rob laughed out loud, "What do you think of Captain Frank's special sauce?"

Elaine's eyes were still watering. "My gosh... How can he drink that stuff all the time?"

Rob took another sip and answered, "Not really sure, but I do know one thing... I haven't had to zip up my jacket yet."

Elaine wiped the water from her eyes just before it started to trickle down her cheek. "I don't think the alcohol is warming you. I'm pretty sure you're just too numb to feel the chill."

Rob chuckled. "You might be right."

Elaine asked, "Did you notice Whitney in there tonight?"

"No, but then again... I wasn't paying attention to anyone. Why?"

"Every time I looked up, she was staring at one of us at our table," Elaine said. "There's something about that woman I just can't figure out."

Rob looked out over the bay. "Do you think the network sent her to size us up, or she's just checking us out for herself?"

Elaine glanced at Rob. "I don't know. She's rooming with us, and yet she only hangs out with them. Like the other night when she left our room and went down to their quarters, remember? You met her at the door?"

Rob answered, "Yeah, I remember."

As if on cue, the door to the deck opened, and out came Whitney. She closed the door and started making her way to the bow. Rob looked at Elaine and said, "Well, here comes Whitney. Maybe it's time to have a little chat with her."

Whitney walked past Elaine to the other side of Rob. "Hey, guys, can we talk in private for a minute?" she asked.

"We were just thinking the same thing," Rob said.

Elaine spoke next, "I was just explaining to Rob about dinner. Why were you staring at us throughout the meal?"

"I don't know for sure," Whitney replied. She continued, "For one thing, I'm intrigued by this place and all of you. Secondly, I want each of you to know that I am on your side."

Elaine asked, "What do you mean...our side?"

"I believe your account of everything that took place a year ago. I can also sense we are not alone here," answered Whitney.

"But?" Rob asked.

Whitney looked Rob in the eye. "I've never met any of these other people, not even Joe Wilburn from the network. And you've never met the man?"

Rob answered, "No, but then again, I've never met you either."

Whitney grinned. "That's true. I have never met you, Rob. But I have heard of you. Never heard of a Joe Wilburn before, though."

Elaine asked, "What about the two from the insurance company?"

Whitney slightly raised her hands. "Couldn't tell you one thing about them. I'm still wondering why they are on this little excursion."

Rob asked, "Why do you think they sent you and Joe here?"

Whitney replied, "I think to cover the network's butt, plus it looks good in the public eye if the network contributes to the situation."

"What about the bodyguards?" Elaine asked.

Rob spoke before Whitney could answer, "Yes, what do you know about them?"

"Absolutely nothing personally," Whitney said, "but Wilson Wilkins is a well-known trophy hunter, and David Felder seems to buddy up to him quite well. Brad Easton and Harold Birchfield, I haven't figured out yet, but I think Wilson and David are here to score a kill to add to their resumes."

Rob asked Whitney, "Who got all these people together?"

"Not sure," responded Whitney, "but whoever it was...they were higher up the ole corporate ladder than you, Rob."

Rob turned and leaned his backside against the railing of the ship. He took another sip from the mug, and after the difficult swallow of the ingredients, he said, "Whoever it was, Whitney, they were above the vice president on the ole ladder, because he warned me to be careful. And I think you are right about the bodyguards looking for a trophy kill. I'm just not sure if it's two or all four of them. I overheard some conversations back at the network building, but only two men were talking. I'm not sure if the other two were standing there or not."

Elaine asked, "So, are we really here to bring back the others, or not?"

Whitney tilted her head. "I believe some of us are; the others, I'm not so sure about."

Just as Whitney finished speaking, the ship's cabin door opened. Rob turned to face out over the bay once again. One by one, the guests of the port filed onto the narrow deck leading to the bow, and all continued forward until they joined the three already occupying the area.

Aaron from the insurance company was the first to speak, "Man, it doesn't take long after the sun starts to set for the chill to hit the air."

Harold, the smallest bodyguard, chimed in next, "Not long at all, but you have to admit, there's probably not a prettier view in the world than this."

Everybody on the bow agreed as they swiveled their heads in all directions, taking in all that surrounded the ship they were calling home for the next few days. The day was starting to wind down, and soon darkness would overtake the bay. Shelley shivered a little as she remembered coming down the shoreline, the dampness of the rain. The constant sound of the creature following them was still very fresh in her mind. Alicia took notice of Shelley's facial expressions as she recollected the events of that night. It was obvious that something was running rampant through Shelley's mind, but Alicia wasn't sure what.

Bodyguard Brad Easton interrupted the silence, "Why do you guys think Mark and Willy wouldn't come back?"

Shelley snapped out of her deep thoughts and answered, "I think they had their fill of this place a year ago. Mark seen one of these creatures face to face coming off the mountain, so maybe that was enough for him."

Brad looked at Rob and said, "We are not sure if the fall or the creature killed Andre, are we?"

Rob placed his hand on his chin. "We're not a hundred percent sure.

Both of them apparently tumbled pretty good coming down the mountain. They couldn't determine if Andre's injuries were just from the fall or something else. Mark did say one of the creatures swung its arm and hit him."

Wilson Wilkins tilted his fedora hat to expose the salt and pepper hair that bordered his forehead. "How large did Mark say the creature was?"

"All I ever remember him saying was that it was massive in size," Rob said.

David Felder stated, "There must be several of these Hairy Man creatures. Coming down the shoreline, coming off the mountain, and the activity at the cabins all practically happened simultaneously."

Elaine looked at David. "I think there is a pretty good-sized group of these creatures, but this is their home, and we should respect that. We are the ones who don't belong here."

Everybody could sense the tension in Elaine's voice, especially the members of the party here for the first time. From that point on, the talk on the bow drifted slowly to idle chit chat, and there were no more direct questions aimed toward the survivors. After about another 30 minutes, darkness filled the air, and the group started making their way into the warmth of the interior of the ship. But Shelley took notice of the two bodyguards that lagged behind. After another five minutes, the last two made their way through the cabin door. Everyone was filling a coffee cup or had already done so. The first people to the coffee pot were heading down the corridor to the rooms they occupied. Each person filed into their respective rooms.

The door had barely closed, and Shelley whispered, "Did anyone else notice that David and Wilson were a little slow coming in?" Then she added, "I think Whitney is right... Those two are up to something."

Rob responded, "Yeah, I noticed that also... I don't think they were just enjoying the night air anymore."

Alicia was next to weigh in, "It was hard to tell, but it appeared they were whispering to each other."

Whitney took a look around the room at everybody. "Listen, guys, I just want you to know that I am on your side. Everybody understand?"

Rob said, "Yes, we do, but that's the second time you have brought that up."

"I know that," Whitney said. "I read the reports, and for some reason the creatures spared each of you. I want to make sure you look out for me while we are here. I do not want to be left alone."

Shelley was next to speak, "Whitney, these creatures are indeed real. They are living, breathing things that God put on this great green earth. They have as much right to be here as we do. All of us just want to make sure no harm comes to them. Maybe that's why nobody really wants to believe our story. I can't explain why I feel this way after what they did to the others. But you are right—for some reason they spared the rest of us, and I would like for them to just live their lives out undisturbed."

Whitney responded, "I couldn't agree more. I just want you people to look out for me."

"Don't worry, Whitney," Rob said. "Just stay close to us and stay focused."

Then, everyone sat on the side of their bunk and began to enjoy the coffee they had brought back with them. Mostly, they conversed about the ship and its crew. All were very appreciative of the meals they had eaten so far and the hard work of the crew. Even the tiny bunks were praised for the comfort they provided. After about an hour, the group decided to call it a night, and everybody snuggled into their sleeping bags and drifted to dreamland.

***

Alicia slowly awakened and eventually pushed the tiny button on her ole dependable LCD watch. *1:20 a.m.*, she thought. For a second, she thought about just continuing to occupy the nice, warm spot she was in, but all the coffee was beginning to take its toll. The longer she laid there, the more she realized that a trip to the ship's bathroom was inevitable, and the sooner the better.

Alicia finally gave in and unzipped the sleeping bag. Slowly, she slid out of the warm confines of it and sat on the side of her bunk. She opted to make the trek to the bathroom in her insulated underwear but decided the hiking boots would be a necessity as soon as her feet touched the floor. Alicia exited the room and slowly drifted down the small corridor. Soon, she entered the bathroom and decided it was well worth the effort of getting out of the sleeping bag.

After washing her hands and exiting the bathroom, a ray of light shining through one of the ships' windows caught Alicia's eye. She made her way to the front of the ship being as stealthy as possible in her every movement. As she positioned herself to watch the activities outside, she heard someone whisper her name. Immediately she recognized the voice; it was Captain Frank. The captain motioned for Alicia to move over to his position by his cabin door. The door was half ajar and he was intently watching the two on the deck of the boat.

Alicia carefully made her way to Captain Frank and whispered, "What's going on out there?"

Captain Frank replied, "Not totally sure, but if I was going to guess... I'd say they are looking really hard for something."

"A creature?" Alicia asked.

Captain Frank raised his bushy eyebrows. "That's kinda what I'm thinking. They've been out there for the better part of an hour shining those lights along the shoreline and up around the cabins."

Alicia asked, "Think they've seen anything?"

"Hard to say," Captain Frank said. "Every now and then they seem to concentrate on a single location with both lights."

Alicia asked, "Should we confront them?"

"No, let's just let them do whatever they're doing. Think you can sneak back down the hall to your room?"

Alicia smiled. "Yeah, I can pull that off."

"We don't want them to know we caught them. Tell the others first thing in the morning. We'll see if these two offer up any explanation for tonight or if they keep it a secret."

Alicia patted Captain Frank on the shoulder and quietly made her way down the corridor to her quarters, where she opened and shut the door as gently as possible so as to not disturb anyone. The captain continued to watch the two on the deck for another 15 minutes until they called it a night. Captain Frank retreated into his cabin until he was convinced the two were safely back in their room.

Captain Frank entered the front cabin of the boat and poured some of the flask's contents into his cup, only this time there was no coffee in the mug. He opened the door and stepped onto the deck of the boat. The chilly breeze swept across Captain Frank's face, but he only stood there long enough to take three good sips from the mug. Then, he turned to retreat back into the ship. That's when the captain heard the first *whoop*.

It sounded as though it came from the meadow. Then, another one from the cabins on the hill. Suddenly there was a bellowing howl directly in front of him at the landing site for the rafts. Next came the splash in the water about halfway between the shoreline and the boat. The captain eased his hand onto the set of switches located inside the door and clicked on the vessel's external lights.

There were two pairs of eyes at the landing site staring back at him and another pair close to the cabins. Suddenly they all disappeared, and Captain Frank thought to himself, *They know we are here.*

CHAPTER 10

As daylight came to the bay and the rays of the sun began to make their way down the mountainside, the people on the boat started to stir. The boat's crew had already begun to prepare breakfast. One could already smell the aroma of bacon and coffee throughout the boat. Alicia filled her roommates in on the events that she and Captain Frank witnessed the night before.

Just as Alicia finished, there was a knock on the cabin door and one of the young crew informed the group that breakfast was about to be served. After putting on the finishing touches of their day's attire, Rob opened the cabin door, and the smell of the morning meal became even stronger to the group.

Rob turned to Shelley and said, "I think I could get comfortable with this way of life. Good food and the simple things."

Shelley grinned. "Maybe life back at the fishing port. Not so sure about taking up residence right here in this location."

Rob smiled. "Yeah, back at the village would be nice. Maybe Frank could find me a job, or maybe...work at the airport we flew into."

Shelley pointed a finger at Rob. "I think you could find employment at one of those locations, but how in the world could you make it without the hustle and bustle of show business?"

Rob started laughing as the group made their way to the mess hall.

When they arrived, the others were already sitting at one of the tables with their coffee cups emitting the steam of the morning brew. As the second crew group sat down, the ship's crew started serving the food, which everyone heartily dove into and started consuming.

After the meal was finished, Wilson leaned back in his chair. "Guys, I think we'll search around the cabins today as one group. Hopefully, we can locate Dave and Betty. We'll try to get them on board the ship before spreading out and looking for the others."

Everybody agreed on the plan either by nodding or verbally acknowledging Wilson. They all savored the last of their coffee and returned to their rooms to grab their gear.

In about 15 minutes, the people going ashore assembled on the deck and began the procedure of transferring from the boat to the land. The second group climbed onto the raft as the first one sped off. The loading only took a few minutes, and soon the first raft slid onto the sandy loading zone. After that group was safely on the shore and the raft was back on the way to the boat, the second craft glided onto the land in exactly the same manner. Everyone exited the raft, and they lined up in exactly the same manner as the day before, only this time Wilson was leading the way and Brad was bringing up the rear. As the second raft was on its route back to the ship, the search party began to make their way up the trail. Alicia and Whitney were the only ones to take a second look back.

If anyone had taken the time to survey the landing zone, right behind the small clearing for the landing of the rafts was a large footprint beside two saplings. A footprint left behind from whatever Captain Frank saw the night before.

The small trek up to the cabins only took a few minutes, but it seemed that Wilson and David were being extra cautious this morning. Alicia paid close attention to them as the group traversed the narrow trail guarded by the scrub bushes. She couldn't help but wonder if the men had seen something in the darkness as they searched with their spotlights. Neither had divulged anything about last night's activities. The group turned onto the path that led to the cabins and after reaching the crew's cabin paused at the steps. Wilson slowly made his way to the deck and peered into the space where the front door once stood. Next, he scanned both sides of the cabin as he stared around each corner. Once he was confident the coast was clear, Wilson motioned for everyone to join him, but there seemed to be a totally different mood to the group today.

Bodyguard Harold was the first to offer a plan for today's search: "After we all talked yesterday, we seem to believe that Betty was pulled through the window and attacked on the deck." He walked to the spot on the deck outside the window and took a long look at the dark stains on the wooden planks and outside wall. "If the creature killed Betty here, it would be my guess that it may have thrown her body downhill toward the bay."

A chill ran through Elaine's body when she realized they were now hunting for the remains of the people that occupied this place with her last year. "How do we want to search?" she asked.

Wilson looked around the area and answered, "I think we should place a bodyguard on each of the cabin decks for lookouts, and the other two border the group as they search."

"How about Harold and I stay with the group?" Brad asked, then pointed to Wilson and David. "You guys take the first lookout."

Wilson said, "Sounds good, but everybody stay close and make sure you're in contact with someone else at all times."

Wilson positioned himself at the corner of the deck facing the bay. David made his way to the contestant cabin and positioned himself in the same corner of that deck to observe the others as they searched. The group began to scour the area below the cabins, and step by step they methodically made their way through the thick undergrowth and small bushes. The sun was beaming down, but the unrelentless thickness was making it almost impossible to see anything around them. Each person took their time hoping not to miss a single detail.

Almost as if they were heeding Wilson's advice, every so often each member of the group would look up to make sure they were in close proximity to another person. They continued to move through the area and were about to lose hope when Aaron Nelson from the insurance company spotted a small piece of blue material hanging above his head in a small sapling. The shredded material was hanging on a limb about eight feet in the air, and immediately Aaron knew there was no way it got there by someone just passing by.

Aaron turned to face the others and almost panicked when he realized that nobody was in his sight. He interjected, "Hey, people?"

Brad Easton answered, "Yeah, whatcha got, Aaron?"

Aaron gasped with the relief of hearing Brad's voice. "Does anyone remember what Betty was wearing that night?"

Elaine responded from a position that Aaron couldn't see, "I think she had jeans and a gray shirt on. Maybe she was wearing a light blue jacket also."

Aaron could only hear Elaine's voice. She probably wasn't 50 feet from him, but the dense brush and foliage blocked any view of her. He merely looked in the direction of her voice and said, "I've got a blue piece of material hanging on a tree limb."

Harold chimed in, "Everyone stay put. I'll go to Aaron and check it out."

Aaron could hear the bodyguard's clothing scraping the bushes as he closed in on him. In his mind, Aaron deeply hoped the sound coming in his direction was indeed Harold. Suddenly, Harold came into view, and he could see the look of fear on Aaron's face. "Relax, Aaron, it's just me."

Aaron sighed and shook his head, then pointed to the piece of material in the tree. "There, on the limb."

Harold said, "Yep, that don't belong there." Then, he noticed another tree limb that was broken in another sapling below them. "Down there, looks like something heavy hit that sapling. Let's have a look."

About eight or nine careful steps below them, and the two men were standing beside the broken sapling. Each one of them began to search the area around them. Suddenly, Harold spotted the bottom of a hiking boot. He wrapped his fingers around Aaron's wrist and said, "There's a boot."

Harold released his grip on Aaron and moved toward the boot. Aaron never moved an inch, and the only sound he could hear was his own breathing as he gasped for air. Harold bent down on one knee and slowly moved the foliage from around the shoe. The two had definitely located Betty. He turned to Aaron and nodded yes. Aaron looked to his left and dropped his head.

Harold came to his feet and looked in the direction of the others. "Hey, everybody. We have found Betty."

Even though nobody's face could clearly be seen, all had the same expression of relief and sorrow. Slowly, the others made their way to the two men. Harold had already removed the body bag from his backpack and was zipping it close when they arrived.

Brad looked at Harold. "I'll help you up the hill," he said.

Harold replied, "It's really not that heavy. I would like for you to keep an eye on us going back up the hill."

"Will do," Brad said. As he turned, he noticed a tear gently rolling down Elaine's cheek, and he patted her on the shoulder. "Come on, Elaine, let's go."

Harold wasn't sure how far below the cabins they were, but he knew one thing for sure. It was a long way for something to throw a human being. After several minutes, the group made their way to the smaller bushes that surrounded the cabins, and one by one they navigated to the steps of the crew's cabin. Harold climbed the steps and respectfully laid the bag on the wooden planks of the deck. Everyone else stood in silence on the trail between the two cabins.

After a moment, Wilson said, "People, I know we need to show this person a little respect, but unfortunately we have another to locate."

Harold came to his feet and looked at the others. "Elaine, show us again where you found Dave's arm."

Without saying a word, the group all walked to the contestant cabin and onto the deck. Wilson stood guard at the crew's cabin with vigilance. The group rounded the corner of the cabin and Elaine pointed to the spot where she found the arm. Only Brad and Harold walked to the spot. Both men turned and stared out beyond the railing. They talked to each other as they scanned and pointed.

Finally, Brad faced the group to say, "We think that Dave will most likely be in this direction." Then, he raised his arm to display the area to search.

Brad and Harold walked past the group. All fell in line and started heading to the search area. As Shelley got to the steps, she glanced at Betty's remains. Just as Shelley began to go down the steps, something caught her eye, and she stopped dead in her tracks.

Shelley firmly said, "Elaine."

The group halted, and Elaine answered, "What, Shelley?"

Shelley pointed. "The railing... There are more stones."

Elaine almost knocked Whitney down the hill as she made her way back to the top of the steps. "How could we have missed them earlier?" she asked.

Shelley replied, "I don't know, but there they are, all lined up in a row on the railing."

"How many are there?" Ronnie asked.

Elaine turned to Ronnie. "Ten."

Jeff from the insurance company said, "That doesn't make any sense. You guys said there was a stone for each person at the cabins last year."

Joe from the network said, "Jeff's right. There's...what? Thirteen of us here right now."

Shelley asked, "Nobody saw any stones here yesterday, right?"

Everyone confirmed that they didn't see them the day before, then Rob said, "They had to be placed on the railing after we went back to the boat."

In his mind, Wilson confirmed the suspicion that he and David had seen something near the cabins last night. "They are right, Elaine," Wilson said. "There are thirteen of us, and only ten stones."

Elaine looked to the other deck of the crew cabin at Wilson. "Something put these rocks here just like last year. Why there are only ten, I don't know."

Brad spoke next, "You guys stated that the number changed from one to two, then fourteen to thirteen. I say we find Dave, get him and Betty back to the boat, and tomorrow we'll check the stones again before searching for the others."

Elaine and Shelley nodded and joined the others. They moved to the side of the cabin and began the search. This time, they remained at arm's length as they moved through the foliage and underbrush. Wilson continued to survey everything around the crew cabin, and David remained on the side deck facing the search party. At times, he could only see one or two of the group, and this made him feel very uneasy. David knew that if something happened, there was no way he could provide the protection they needed. In his mind, Wilson was completely sure that something was watching; he just couldn't figure out from where. Wilson didn't like the fact that two of them were out in the open and the rest were buried in the thickness beyond the cabins.

Suddenly, there was a loud shriek somewhere in the group. David raised his weapon and struggled to make sense of what was going on. Next came the sound of something moving in the dense area. There was a moment of panic for David on the deck until he heard Brad's voice call out, "Everything's okay. I believe we have found Dave."

Whitney turned to face away from what was left of Dave. He, too, was mostly bones wrapped in the remnants of the clothing he wore on that fateful night. Elaine made her way to Whitney and wrapped her arms around the other woman. They stepped back as Harold approached.

Harold knelt down beside Brad and said, "His skull is crushed the same way that Mark and Willy described the people at the old homestead."

Brad tilted his head and looked at Harold. "Yeah, it took a lot of force to do this. Let's get him in the bag and get back to the cabins. I really don't like being in this dense stuff and not feeling capable of seeing something if it attacked us."

Brad removed the body bag from his backpack that he was carrying, and they placed the remains inside. Brad zipped the bag. Elaine turned loose of Whitney and grabbed a strap handle on one end of the bag. Brad picked up the other end, and Elaine said, "Let's get out of here."

Harold told the group to head back and waited for everyone to line up and start walking. He took a quick look around but could see absolutely nothing in the dense foliage. Just a few steps into their exit, there was a crashing sound from above the group. It seemed to be approaching at a fast rate covering a large distance with each thump as it impacted the ground. Harold had the weapon in a ready position to greet whatever was coming at them when it suddenly stopped, and everyone stood perfectly still.

Jeff Sizemore whispered, "What was that?"

Nobody answered; they simply used their eyes to scan every direction. After a couple of minutes, Harold nodded for the group to continue, it took several minutes for the searchers to break out of the thick underbrush and move to the path at the cabins.

Once David finished the head count of the group, he asked, "Did you guys hear that above you?"

Harold replied, "Sure did, buddy, but it just stopped and never moved again."

Ronnie wiped the sweat from his forehead. "Sounded like a rock coming down the hill."

"A rock?" Joe Wilburn asked.

Ronnie turned to Joe and shook his head. "Yes, apparently these things like to throw rocks...happened last year, too."

Wilson interrupted, "Let's get these two back to the boat. We'll come up with some ideas about tomorrow."

Elaine and Brad still held the bag with Dave's remains. Ronnie and Aaron picked up Betty. Wilson positioned himself at the front of the group and Harold brought up the rear. Methodically they made their way down to the loading area. Wilson removed the radio and called for the rafts about halfway down. He informed the captain that they had found Betty and Dave. The search party looked up briefly as they heard the outboard motors fire up, and all felt a small wave of security rush over them from the sound. All were trying to determine if one of the creatures was coming down the hill toward them or if Ronnie was right in that one of them had thrown a large rock in their direction.

Soon, the first raft was loaded and speeding back to the ship. The second raft was being loaded when Wilson noticed the enormous footprint in the soft dirt beside the sapling. Being a big game trophy hunter, he couldn't believe he and David had missed it when unloading this morning. Wilson gripped David's elbow and pointed to the print. David studied the impression for just a second, then winked at Wilson. They were the last two to board the raft, but Rob had noticed the men as they stared at the footprint. He wasn't sure of what the men had seen, but he definitely knew they were intrigued by it.

The second raft backed away from the shore, turned, and headed back to the boat. Betty and Dave were finally going home.

CHAPTER 11

Once back at the boat, Betty and Dave's remains were carried to the holding room set aside for the people that didn't get to leave last year. The members of the search party made their way to their respective rooms to get cleaned up before dinner. In the cabin room occupied by the support group assembled by the network, some sat on the sides of their bunks while others stood and seemed to stare into a dark void.

Finally, Jeff from the insurance company turned around and faced the group. "What do you make of all that commotion coming down the hill, Harold?"

Harold was sitting on his bunk looking down at the floor. "I'm not sure... At first, I thought something was charging down the hill toward us, but maybe Ronnie's right.

Joe from the network said, "Listen, people. I have been skeptical of the entire situation from a year ago, probably the biggest skeptic of everybody here. But now... Well, I'm not so sure that there isn't something here."

Insurance representative Aaron spoke next, "I know we were not only brought here to retrieve the others but also to confirm the survivors' story, but I don't believe any of last year's survivors could have possibly inflicted the injuries of the two people we found today."

Bodyguard Brad wheeled on a dime, "Are you telling me the network and insurance company sent you guys up here to confirm the testimonies of these people? Is this some kind of a witch hunt or something?"

Aaron shook his head. "No, we weren't —"

Brad interjected, "Good gosh, people!" Then, he looked at David Felder and said, "What exactly is going on here?"

"All I know," David began, "is that we were hired to come up here and protect these individuals of the search party." Which was only partially the truth, since he and Wilson had another motive for coming to the port.

Aaron said, "The representatives of the network and the insurance company just want proof of everything that took place here a year ago. At least, that was the information I was told."

Harold chimed in next, "Just exactly what kind of proof are they looking for?"

Joe Wilburn said, "They want to verify the injuries of the deceased and see if they match what Mark and Willy described at the homestead."

Brad ran his fingers through his hair. "For crying out loud... They examined Sasha and Tim. Did that not confirm the stories they told? Surely the reps don't think these survivors went rogue and killed the others. I really don't think one of these people have the strength to do that kind of damage to Dave Murrows' skull or rip one of his arms off."

Jeff placed his hands out in front of his waist. "We're not blaming any of the survivors. We are all here just trying to determine what this animal was that killed these people. Maybe it was a bear... You know good and well that when we heard something coming from above us, nobody could see anything."

Brad responded, "That's true, but Elaine and Mark have both seen these creatures, and Elaine even interacted with them. Do you think she was so delirious that she gave first aid to a bear? Come on. Elaine looked these things directly in the eye."

"I don't know exactly what Elaine did," Aaron admitted. "We have her account of the events, but nobody else saw her interactions. Fear does a lot of things to people."

Harold looked Aaron in the eye and said, "What did fear do to you today after we found Dave and started back? Did you see a bear, or maybe even a Hairy Man?"

Aaron dropped his head. "I didn't see anything."

"What did you feel?" Harold asked.

Aaron looked back up. "I was afraid."

"I think we all were," Harold said. "I know I was, and I had a weapon. I also believe that these survivors encountered the same creature as the people did over 75 years ago. Maybe one of them threw a rock at us. There was definitely something crashing through the brush. I just don't know what it was."

David Felder interrupted, "Speaking of that... I didn't have a visual on each of you guys while the search was going on. We need to make sure that we can provide cover for everybody at all times."

Wilson stood from the side of his bunk. "Absolutely. Even when we separate into the two groups tomorrow, each group needs to be fully protected by the bodyguards."

Joe asked reluctantly, "Do we really need to separate?"

Wilson answered, "It'll make the recovery process go a little quicker. The sooner we find the others, the sooner we are out of here."

Everyone in the room agreed and began to put away their gear. Now, there was a lot of suspicion in everybody's mind about the role of each person in the cabin room they all occupied. All but Wilson and David. They had their own plan for proving what had terrified the group a year ago.

Suddenly, there was a knock at the other cabin door. Rob opened it, and Captain Frank squeezed by him as he entered the room. Rob closed the door, and the captain looked around the room. "How did it go out there today?"

Alicia answered first, "Well, for one thing, nobody from next door mentioned last night's activity."

Next, Captain Frank moved his eyes to focus on Whitney and looked back at Shelley, who grinned and said, "It's okay, Captain. The best we can tell, Whitney is on our side."

Captain Frank turned and faced Whitney. "Do we know the motives of the people in the other room?"

Whitney just shook her head. "I really don't know anything about any of them, but I have suspicions about some or all of the bodyguards. I have never met Joe from the network or the insurance people."

Captain Frank said, "I'm assuming Alicia filled you guys in on the two individuals outside last night?"

Everybody nodded yes, then the captain added, "It was hard to tell, but I'm pretty sure it was Wilson and David, and they were searching pretty hard with those spotlights."

"I'm thinking they may have their own plan for proving the existence of this creature," Rob added.

"Couldn't tell for sure, but I don't think either of them had a weapon last night on the ship's deck," Captain Frank said.

Shelley said, "They got something up their sleeve."

Captain Frank replied, "Not sure if they spotted anything or not...but we did have company watching us from the shore."

Rob adjusted his stance. "Think so?"

The captain lifted his mug and took a swig. "Oh... I know so. After Alicia made her way down the corridor, I continued to spy on the others, and after a few minutes they came in and retired for the night. I eased outside to take a quick look around and grab some fresh air. That's when I heard the two vocalizations. Been a long time since I heard that sound. A lot of years have passed since me and my buddies spent that night on the boat in this bay. I turned on the boat's outside lights, and you could see the eyes shining from the shore."

Rob asked, "Where were they?"

Captain Frank answered, "There were two pair next to the landing area for the rafts. It was hard to tell, but it looked like another pair up next to the cabins."

Rob nodded his head and said, "That might explain what Wilson and David were looking at when we were boarding the raft. They took a long, hard look at something on the ground...maybe some tracks."

"You are probably right about the cabins," Shelley said. "There are more stones on the railing of the contestant cabin."

Captain Frank took a quick glance down at his mug, then focused back on the group. "I don't like this, guys. I'm not sure if you people should go back ashore or not."

"We have to locate the others and bring them back home," Elaine said sternly. "Plus, we have to protect these creatures that live here."

Captain Frank took a deep breath. "Just get the others, Elaine. What lives here can take care of itself."

Captain Frank exited the room, and Whitney sat down on her bunk. "Why only ten stones?" she asked.

"I'm kinda confused about that, too," Rob said. "There's thirteen of us on this recovery mission that are going ashore."

Elaine answered, "Three of us already have stones."

Whitney had a look of confusion on her face. "Are you telling me these things remember you three from last year? Are they that intelligent?"

Elaine smiled. "I believe so. I was thinking about it while we were searching for Dave. That's the only explanation I could come up with; it's the only thing that makes sense."

Rob said, "So, these creatures recognize you, Ronnie, and Shelley?"

Ronnie responded, "I think Elaine is right, which means they have probably been watching us since the minute we arrived."

Whitney gasped. "Oh my gosh! Why haven't they done anything yet if they have been that close?"

Shelley answered, "They have... One of them placed the stones on the railing and another has hurled a stone down the hillside at us."

Whitney asked, "And just what do these things mean?"

Ronnie said, "They're just letting us know that they are there and keeping an eye on us. It wouldn't have been a problem for these creatures to have rushed us at a moment's notice today, but they are trying to feel out what our purpose in being here is."

Elaine said, "As long as we continue to recover the others, everything will be okay, but if one of the others stray from that objective, there may be trouble."

Then, Shelley pointed her finger at Rob, Alicia, and Whitney to say, "You three need to be in constant contact with one of us at all times... Okay?"

The three of them nodded, and Ronnie turned to Alicia. "I don't suppose there's a chance I could talk you into staying on the boat tomorrow?"

Alicia grinned. "Not a chance. I go where you go, big boy."

"I figured that was going to be your answer," Ronnie said. "I don't know what I was thinking. It ain't like you ever listen to me."

The entire group laughed, and Shelley said, "Aah, the joys of married life."

They all began to laugh even harder, and Alicia slapped Ronnie on the shoulder. Then, they began to prepare for the evening's meal. Soon they were all walking down the corridor to the mess hall along with the group from the other quarters. Tonight's meal consisted of potato soup accompanied by golden cornbread cooked in real iron skillets. All heartily enjoyed the meal that had been prepared for them. After everyone was finished, Wilson asked Rob if they could study the map again. Rob answered yes and left to retrieve the paper. The others sat silently in their seats or just idly milled around in the room until Rob returned. He unfolded the map, which once again revealed the layout of the area. Wilson slowly ran his fingers over the laminated document starting at the cabins and moving toward the homestead the group had investigated nearly a year ago.

Wilson looked up at Rob. "You said there was a GPS position for Mr. Long?"

Rob answered, "Yes, Mark and Andre used the monitor to locate the beacon. Once they found the tracking beacon and Mr. Long, Mark saved the coordinates on the monitor."

Wilson said, "Great, we should be able to take a GPS device with us and go directly to the spot. I would like to write down the Lat and Long measurements so there are no questions when we get out there."

Almost on cue, one of the young crew members opened a cabinet door, removed a pen and small paper pad, and placed them on the table at the two men. Once again, Rob left the room as everybody continued to study the map. Just a couple of minutes later, he returned and sat down beside Wilson. He opened a small binder book and began to flip pages, and soon he found the information he was searching for and placed his finger on it.

"There it is, the latitude and longitude of the transmitter," Rob said.

Wilson slid the tablet in front of himself, and as he began to write the coordinates down, he said, "This should make locating Mr. Long a lot easier, but I'm afraid Sandy and Bill are going to be more of a challenge."

Shelley adjusted herself on the bench-like seat. "When Ronnie and I heard the gunshot, we were still in the meadow. But it sure sounded like it came from the spot where we left the old, abandoned road to investigate the meadow."

Bodyguard Brad asked, "Do you think that the two of you can find that spot again?"

"Oh, no doubt," Shelley said. "There's kinda a trail that leaves the road, goes down a bank, and heads for the meadow and stream."

Brad said, "My guess is that is where we should start."

David Felder turned to Ronnie to ask, "How far is it to the meadow?"

Ronnie answered, "It's a pretty good hike, but the terrain is good for walking. I couldn't tell you the exact distance, because that was a year ago and we only made the trek a couple of times."

Brad said, "But we will be able to get up there, do our searching, and get back well before dark?"

Ronnie responded, "Oh yeah. The first day we went to the meadow and looked around, we got back in plenty of time before dark."

Wilson interrupted, "If we can locate Mr. Long rather quickly, maybe we can assist you guys with finding Bill and Sandy. If need be, we can all go as a group on the second trip up there and search together...depending on your success tomorrow."

David Felder said, "Sounds like a good idea... We'll see how tomorrow goes. I would also like to find Mr. Long's shelter and retrieve his personal belongings. Apparently he carried some family pictures with him when he traveled on his expeditions. Might be kind of nice if we could return them also."

Wilson took a long look around the room for the reactions of the others, but for now there were none. He said, "We'll find the others first; that is our number one priority. After we do that, nobody is under any further obligation. David and I will retrieve Mr. Long's belongings."

Rob looked at Wilson. "I just want to find the others and get out of this place. If you and David want to retrieve his belongings, that's up to you."

Wilson dropped his head to once again look at the map. "The network person that spoke to me just said that Mr. Long's family would like to have his stuff if possible, I'm guessing for sentimental reasons. I told him that we would not risk the safety of the group, but David and I would go get his stuff if time allowed. Do we know exactly the location of the stand?"

Rob flipped back some pages of the book until he found the coordinates written down at the bottom of a page. "Right here," he said.

Wilson wrote down the latitude and longitude of the stand, folded the piece of paper, and placed it in the left-hand pocket of his shirt. "We better get some rest, people. Tomorrow's gonna be a busy day."

Rob folded the map some, grabbed another cup of coffee, and all retreated to their cabin rooms on the boat.

Once the door to their cabin was closed, Whitney said, "That's the first time I've heard anything about Mr. Long's belongings."

"Yes, that makes two of us," Rob said.

Elaine nodded. "Sounds like the two of them want to get out there alone."

Alicia said, "I think that confirms that it was them two on the deck of the boat last night with the spotlights."

"No doubt about it," Shelley said. "Did anyone notice the other bodyguards?"

Everybody looked at Shelley, then she raised her eyebrows and said, "I think that ole Wilson and David were trying to see what reaction they were gonna get out of us. I don't think they even considered what the other bodyguards' reactions would be."

Rob asked, "And just what was their reaction?"

Shelley replied, "They had a look of confusion on their faces. Brad even squinted his eyes as he looked at Harold."

Rob exhaled a large breath, "Maybe they didn't know about the mementos of Mr. Long... I sure wasn't informed of anything like that."

Elaine said, "Sounds like they want to go on a little hunting trip. I think their plan is to bring one of the creatures' bodies back for proof and self-glory. If I have anything to do with it, that ain't never gonna happen."

"How are we gonna stop it?" Shelley asked.

Elaine stared into Shelley's eyes. "I'll do whatever it takes. We have weapons, too."

Rob sat on the side of his bunk. "Elaine... You can't just shoot one or both of them guys."

Ronnie was the next to speak, "I don't think it'll come to that, Rob. Mr.

Long, Mark, Bill, and Tim all had weapons, and these creatures outsmarted them. I think the captain is right—all we need to worry about is ourselves. These so-called Hairy Man creatures can take care of themselves."

A million things were running through Whitney's mind, then all of a sudden, she asked, "Wait a minute... You guys got weapons?"

Everybody turned to face Whitney and collectively answered, "Yes."

"Don't you think one of you people could have let me in on that little secret?" asked Whitney.

Rob shrugged. "Well, we weren't totally sure about your role in all of this."

Whitney smiled. "Well, at least I chose the right side to be on."

Everyone grinned and began to prepare for the night's rest. Soon, the lights were out and each of them were zipped up snugly in their sleeping bags. Mostly, it was a restless night with a lot of tossing and turning.

CHAPTER 12

Morning came all too quickly for those who didn't sleep well. The skies were covered with a thin layer of clouds, and the air in the bay was a little breezy. Nonetheless, everybody emerged from the warm sleeping bags and began to prepare themselves for the day's search. They donned their pants and shirts over the insulated underwear they had slept in the night before. Slowly and methodically, each person slid their feet into the hiking boots which they laced to meet the standard of comfort they desired. There was not a lot of conversation in either of the cabin rooms, just the occasional moan or groan of rendering themselves ready to attack the day.

Soon all were in the mess hall, and after exchanging the usual morning greetings they began to eat the breakfast prepared by the crew. It appeared everyone was deciphering the events to come for the day in their own minds. As soon as everyone was finished, Wilson asked, "Everybody ready to get started?"

The entire room nodded, and he added, "Well, let's get a move on."

They returned to their respective rooms and grabbed the last of the gear they needed for the day's search. Everyone made their way to the launching deck for the rafts. Everyone boarded the rafts and proceeded to the landing area exactly as it had occurred for the last two mornings. As soon as the last raft began its trip back to the ship, they assembled into single file formation and started heading up the trail to the cabins on the hill.

About halfway up the trail, Wilson abruptly came to a stop; it didn't take long for the smell to travel its way down to the end of the formation. The musky odor was detectable by each and every one of them. Right away, Shelley noticed the smell was not as strong as the moment the creature closed in on her and Ronnie. But there was definitely no denying what the smell was—that damp, musky odor would be something she would never forget.

The four bodyguards took extra time to scan the area for possible threats, and finally Shelley spoke, "Guys, that smell would be a lot stronger if one was really close...and being stuck on this path between this thick foliage is not our best option."

Wilson almost scolded Shelley for not letting them do their job, but thought better of it. "You're probably right, Shelley, let's get to the top of this trail."

Once the group reached the spot where the trail broke off to go to last year's cabins, Jeff Sizemore asked, "So, did that odor coming up the trail belong to one of the creatures?"

Elaine answered, "Yes, but Shelley is right... That pungent odor would have been a lot worse if one had actually been close by. It does tell us one thing, though—there's been one pretty close to this spot at some point and time since yesterday."

Aaron turned to look at Elaine. "Just how close?"

Once again, Elaine was quick to answer, "Probably real close. Maybe right on this path. Listen, people, don't think for a minute that these things don't know we are here. They've been watching us ever since the boat pulled into this bay, and they will keep watching us until we are gone. Do not deviate from our plan of retrieving the bodies."

Joe Wilburn glanced out over the bay. "Just find the others and take them to the boat, right?"

Ronnie responded this time, "Right. We find the others and get out of here. If Elaine is right on her compassion theory, we should be okay."

Aaron Nelson shifted his eyes to see Ronnie. "Should be?"

Even though Aaron was still looking at Ronnie, Elaine was the one to answer, "We are the intruders here, Aaron."

Wilson spoke next, "Hopefully, we can find the remaining three today, then tomorrow David and I will retrieve Mr. Long's belongings. As soon as that happens, we are out of here."

Harold Birchfield addressed the group, "Let's split up and go locate these people. If anything happens, just holler on the handheld radios."

All the bodyguards removed their radios and clipped them on one of the front straps of their backpacks. The group made the short trek to the old, abandoned road and silently divided into the two search parties they had agreed on earlier on the ship. Each group wished the other good luck, and they were off.

Rob, Elaine, Whitney, Aaron, Harold, and Wilson started down the road to search for Mr. Long.

Shelley, Ronnie, Alicia, Joe, Jeff, Brad, and David took a right turn, then they started the trek toward the meadow.

It didn't take but a minute for the two groups to realize they were completely isolated from one another. Harold turned to take one last look at the other group, but they had already disappeared into the thickness of the area. Wilson led his group slowly down the road, steadily scanning both sides and directly in front of him. So far there was nothing to see but the occasional bird darting from tree to tree. Wilson didn't care for the overcast skies and how dark it made the forest. But at least there was no sunlight shining through the trees to cast shadows, he thought. Shadows can really play tricks on one's eyes. After several minutes, Wilson held out his hand to halt the group. Everybody froze, expecting the worst.

Wilson knelt on one knee and turned to the group. "Let's take five, people."

Whitney let out a sigh of relief, and Elaine patted her on the forearm.

Wilson removed his pack and unzipped it; next he pulled out the GPS device and turned it on. After acquiring satellites, it gave him the exact latitude and longitude of their location. He unbuttoned his khaki shirt and removed the piece of paper that he had written Mr. Long's location on. Wilson turned to the group and said, "Looks like we still need to go down the road a little before we start up the mountain. Everybody doing okay?"

Some only nodded, and some verbally whispered yes. Everyone was very attentive to their surroundings. Wilson gave the group closer to 10 minutes before he stood and motioned for the group to continue. The progress going down the road was slow and steady. Harold kept a close eye out behind the group to ensure nothing caught them off guard from that direction.

The road behind the cabins that led to the meadow consisted of several switchbacks before it met the edge of the forest. The so-called clearing was really just tall grass littered with several saplings and scrub bushes. David Felder was leading the search party, while Brad Easton guarded the rear. Brad was uneasy with the feeling of not being able to see more than five feet on either side of the road into the clearing. The thought of something charging out of the grass and attacking them before he could properly react kept running through his mind.

For the moment, all Brad could do was to continue to follow. He would swing his weapon from side to side, much like a soldier trying to clear a building. Little did they know, the group had already walked past the remains of Sandy hidden in the tall grass above the road.

Finally, the group reached the tree line, and David instructed the members of the party to take a breather. Everyone turned to look back at the cabins. Over the top of the cabins, they could plainly see the boat resting on the waters of the bay. Ronnie could remember the view quite well. The last time he was here, he had Stan hoisted across his shoulder.

Shelley broke the silence, "I'll never forget this view and what it felt like to see those cabins."

Ronnie never stopped looking at the boat as he said, "Me neither, Shelley."

Then, they all turned and continued the trek up the road into the dimly lit forest. It took several minutes for each person's eyes to adjust to the new environment they had just entered. They continued to move slowly up the road until David came to a sudden halt. Ronnie reacted a little too slowly and bumped into Alicia. She turned and grabbed Ronnie's arm to keep from tumbling to the ground. Brad stepped out to the right of everyone to see what had caught David's eye.

Joe Wilburn stood perfectly still; his heart was racing to the point where he believed it would jump completely out of his chest. His breaths were coming in rapid pants, and now he was questioning why he was even here. David, hearing Joe's breathing, turned and said, "Easy, Joe... Calm down. There's just some kind of structure up ahead that looks out of place."

Shelley and Ronnie immediately knew what David was staring at. Shelley stepped to the left and looked around at the others. "That's the shelter the creature placed over Ronnie, Stan, and I." Then, she added, "I'm surprised it's still in that good of shape, especially after this amount of time."

Shelley stepped around David and began to move toward the structure. David didn't try to stop her or move back in front of Shelley. He merely flanked Shelley as she made her way up the road to the shelter. He only walked beside her, keeping an eye on the forest around them.

Jeff Sizemore looked at Ronnie and said, "The creature made this to cover you guys?"

Ronnie stepped around Alicia. "Yeah, but the last thing I remember is being laid on the road. When I woke up or regained consciousness the next morning, we were inside this thing, the sun was shining, and the birds were chirping. It was almost like nothing had ever happened."

Joe Wilburn asked, "And after you guys climbed out of this shelter, you just simply walked back to the cabins? I mean, nothing else happened?"

Ronnie answered, "Nope, we put Stan up on my shoulder and as you said, we simply walked back to the cabins."

Everyone stood there staring at the shelter—all except Brad and David, who would only glance at it briefly then return to full-on guard mode. It was only after a couple of seconds that Shelley suddenly realized how quiet it had become in the forest. The silence hadn't registered with the others as they studied the makeshift shelter.

Shelley whispered to Ronnie, "Notice anything, Ronnie?"

Ronnie answered, thinking she was referring to the shelter, "Like what?"

Shelley responded, "There are no birds chirping; the silence is deafening."

All the members of the party began to look around the forest, scanning the forest above and below the road. There was an uneasy feeling that overcame each and every one of them. It was as though they could feel something watching their every move. After several seconds, David Felder turned and faced the others, and he motioned for the group to continue toward the grassy meadow.

It had taken Wilson a little longer than he had anticipated, but the group finally reached the point on the road where they needed to start up the mountain. "Okay, people, according to the GPS, this is where we leave the road. Let's take another five... Then, we'll start the climb."

Aaron Nelson asked, "Do we have an idea of how far up the mountain we got to go?"

Rob responded, "From what Mark said in his report, it's not a terribly long hike, but the first part is really steep before it turns into a gradual climb."

Wilson noted that Aaron didn't look like he had ever spent much time outdoors, let alone climbing up the side of a mountain. Wilson said, "We'll just take our time. Harold and I will keep a lookout... You guys concentrate on your footing."

Whitney lifted her head and looked at Elaine, who sensed the concern on her face. "It'll be okay, Whitney," Elaine said. "I'll be right behind you."

Whitney smiled, and the group came to their feet. Immediately, walking became more difficult as they started the climb to Mr. Long. At times, every person would have to grab onto the saplings to help in the struggle on the advancement up the mountain. Every now and then, someone would slip and inadvertently lose the little ground they had fought so hard to gain.

The resting periods had become more frequent, and each time they stopped, all one could hear was the sucking in and exhaling of air. More often than he liked, Wilson would have to come to a halt for some of the group to recuperate. Finally, he could see the forest opening up a little above them. Wilson stopped and leaned against a small tree. "I think right up there is the spot Mark was talking about. Looks like it opens up some and hopefully ain't as steep."

Aaron was gasping for air, and the sweat was running down his face. "I don't think I can make it all the way up to Mr. Long."

Wilson glanced down to Aaron and said, "We'll take a few more minutes before we start again."

Aaron just dropped his head and stared at the forest floor; he was already conjuring in his mind an excuse not to continue the climb. Rob could sense that Aaron was not going to finish the journey, so he turned to Elaine and raised his eyebrows. After a few more minutes, they started the final push up the steep part of the climb. About 20 yards from the transition area of the mountain, Aaron lost his footing and faceplanted into the leaves. The group halted again as Rob assisted Aaron as he rolled over and came to rest against a tree.

Aaron wiped the dirt and sweat from his face. "Okay, that's it for me... I'll be waiting on you people when you come back down."

Elaine removed her hands from her knees and stood erect. "No... We got to stick together."

Aaron replied, "Listen, Elaine... I'm only slowing the group down. If I keep going, I might have a heart attack, and then there's going to be another person to get back to the boat. I read the report. It's not far to Mr. Long from here... I'll rest right here and just maybe I can help with getting Mr. Long back to the boat."

Elaine started to object, but Wilson interrupted her, "Aaron's right, Elaine. According to the report and the GPS device, Mr. Long is just right up here. We won't be far enough apart that Aaron can't holler if he needs us. Harold or I can assist him in just a couple of seconds."

Elaine looked at Wilson and cocked her head to one side. Wilson imitated the head movement and slightly nodded. The group began to move again, and within a few minutes, they reached the crest of the climb. Rob turned to look at Aaron, who now had reclined into a laying position on the steep slope.

The progress increased dramatically until Wilson stopped and checked the GPS device again. He said, "This should be really close, people. Spread out and see what you can find. But make sure you stay in visual contact with each other, and if you don't mind, Harold, keep an eye out in Aaron's direction."

Harold turned and noticed that he could see the section of the mountain where it began to decline sharply, but Aaron was not visible to him. "Roger that," he said.

Everybody began to mill around as best as they could while focusing on anything that might look like it didn't belong on the forest floor, then Whitney heard a strange sound as her hiking boot collided with something hidden by the leaves. She slowly began to shuffle the leaves with her right foot. Suddenly, the object became visible, and Whitney raised her hand.

"Hey, guys," she said. "I got something here."

Whitney leaned over and lifted the object from the forest floor where it had laid for nearly a year. Right away, Rob recognized what she had in her hand. "That's a pair of night vision goggles," he said. "Mr. Long had a set of them to see in the darkness."

Wilson surveyed the area. "This must be the spot... Let's keep looking."

It only took a few more minutes until Rob leaned onto a large, downed tree and focused his eyes on the other side of the tree. He spied a piece of material protruding from underneath last year's fallen leaves. Rob slowly scanned the spot and noticed other pieces of the material lying slightly hidden in and around the leaves. He said, "I believe we have found Mr. Long."

Everybody stood in their respective positions while Wilson approached Rob. Wilson peered over the tree for just a second and looked at Rob. "I think you're right. Let's move these leaves and see what we got."

It didn't take much effort at all to prove that they had indeed located Mr. Long. Rob and Wilson both knelt down beside the body. Wilson removed the covering that Mark had placed over Mr. Long. Rob was the first to speak, "Even though I heard Mark's account of finding Mr. Long, I never dreamed there was this much damage to the skull."

Elaine made her way over to the tree and studied the skeleton. "That took a lot of force, guys. It looks like he was in a vise or something."

Wilson lifted his head and looked at Elaine. "Maybe the creature placed a hand on each side of the head and squeezed. Do you think one of the big ones you saw could possibly inflict this kind of injury?"

Elaine turned her head away from Mr. Long and slowly scanned the forest. "I think so... Look at what happened to Sasha, Betty, and Dave. I guess it's possible that some of these things could be even larger than the ones I saw. Possibly the only one that could answer your question is lying there in the leaves, and I hate to think what he saw in his last moments."

Wilson removed his backpack and retrieved the body bag. Rob and Wilson carefully placed Mr. Long into the bag.

CHAPTER 13

It had taken several minutes for the second group to traverse up the old road. They finally arrived at the spot where one would turn down the bank to go to the grassy meadow. There had been no surprises, but everyone was still on edge. The entire area had become deathly quiet.

David Felder turned to Ronnie and Shelley. He said, "This is the spot where you left the road?"

Ronnie answered, "Yes, right down the bank to that trail. It connects to the meadow and the stream."

David asked, "Do you think this is where the shot came from?"

"The best we could tell, it was somewhere close to this spot," Shelley said.

Bodyguard Brad said, "So, quite possibly, somewhere close is where Bill and Sandy ran into trouble."

David said, "Yeah, but we don't know if they maybe made it down the road a little or not." David then took a long look around the group. "We'll have to start here and expand our search as necessary. This could prove to be a little more difficult than we imagined."

Everybody started to search the forest floor and look for clues close by, then David said, "We are going to have to spread out some. Just make sure you always are in contact with someone else."

The group began to wander in all directions. Slowly, they moved with their eyes focused on the ground, periodically glancing up to make visual contact with another person.

David, Ronnie, Alicia, and Shelley had moved in position below the road and were busy scouring the forest floor looking for anything that would aid in the location of Bill or Sandy. Brad had climbed the small bank that bordered the road, while Joe Wilburn and Jeff Sizemore searched the old road itself. Joe was watching above and below the road a lot more than helping in the search, and Jeff was busy taking his walking stick and shuffling the leaves back and forth.

Finally, out of sheer luck, Jeff's walking stick came into contact with something hidden under the leaves. Jeff knelt on both knees and moved the leaves aside. Much to his surprise, he had uncovered a pistol that had already started to rust after being exposed to these harsh elements. But nonetheless, it was a pistol, and it was lying beside the road. He felt a rush of satisfaction knowing just maybe he had finally contributed something to the search. Jeff didn't realize how far he and Joe had wandered down the road, and suddenly the satisfaction was replaced with fear. Jeff was intently looking in the direction of Brad when he appeared from behind a large tree quite a way up the road.

Jeff let out a big sigh, "Hey, Brad... I got a pistol here."

Brad clumsily slid down the embankment and made his way up to Jeff. He looked down at the pistol and patted Jeff's shoulder. "Good job, buddy." Brad walked to the side of the road and searched the woods for the people below the road. He spotted David next to the edge of the trees that bordered the meadow. "David, Jeff has found a pistol...probably Bill's pistol."

David took a couple of steps before he could see Brad. Then, he said, "I think we are in the right spot, so keep looking."

Shelley turned to Ronnie and shook her head. "These people are spreading out way too much."

As Alicia made her way along the side of the mountain, she stepped on a small tree limb that had fallen some time back and was hidden under the leaves. Before she had the chance to grab ahold of anything, her feet flew out from under her, and she hit the ground. Ronnie wheeled on a dime. "Alicia, you okay?"

Alicia smiled. "Nothing hurt but my pride."

Ronnie made his way over to Alicia, and while brushing the leaves off of her clothing, he noticed the bone lying in the dirt where she had fallen. "Looks like you found a clue, honey."

Alicia looked down and gasped. "Oh no, Ronnie! Could that be...?"

Alicia turned her head and stepped a few feet to the left as Ronnie addressed the others, "Hey, guys, we got something over here."

David and Shelley approached Ronnie. Alicia was leaning against a large tree facing the meadow. The two of them studied the bone, and David said, "Looks like a human leg bone."

Ronnie replied, "Yeah, I think so."

David scanned the ground. "So, where's the rest of the body?"

Shelley answered, "Got to be close, unless..."

"Unless what?" David asked.

"Unless the person was torn apart like some of the others," Shelley finished.

"Good gosh, people, what kind of a creature is this?"

"A massive territorial creature, David," Ronnie said.

David hollered at Brad up on the road, who appeared in just a couple of seconds. "Yeah, what's up?" Brad asked.

"We think we found a leg bone," David said. "Keep looking above the road and we'll keep searching down here."

Brad just nodded and turned away. He instructed Jeff and Joe to search above the old road. David removed the body bag from his pack and placed the bone in it, and he and the others began to search the leaves more extensively.

The first sign that something might be wrong was when Aaron smelled the odor as he laid back in the leaves. Slowly, he opened his eyes and raised his head to get a sense of direction that the odor was coming from. Since the breeze was coming from his right, it was obvious that something was out the mountain in that direction. He watched the forest, looking for any movement, but there was none. In his mind, Aaron visualized something staring at him, waiting for the right moment to attack. He thought about shouting out to the others, but he wasn't sure how far they were from him, and he didn't want whatever that was producing the smell to know his location.

Aaron's mind was racing at an incredible rate, and his heart was pounding almost as fast as it was coming up the mountain. He could feel the panic that was overtaking his body, and he muttered to himself, "Why am I even out here in this uninhabited place? No, that's not right. Something lives here."

Aaron couldn't determine if something was indeed watching him or not. Now he was thinking he possibly did see things at times when he was staring out the hillside. His breathing had become more like a person who had begun their morning run several minutes ago. The fear was beginning to take its grip. His mind was racing, and the thoughts became more and more confusing to him. As Aaron continued to scan out to his right, he thought to himself, *Should I wait for the others? Should I yell at them? What if the creature is preparing to attack up the mountain? I don't want to be left out here alone.*

Without explanation, in the next few seconds, Aaron was scooting down the mountainside until he was able to plant his feet and come to an upright position. For the next several minutes, he took calculated steps while grasping small saplings to aid in his descent. Then out the mountain to his right came the whooping sound. Aaron slid up to a large pine tree and stopped. He stared out at the mountain intently once again, but he saw nothing. His next move came from sheer panic as he began to move down the mountain in leaps and bounds. Aaron fell numerous times in his hasty retreat, but all he could think of was getting back to the old road, and then making it down to the shoreline.

The group had just secured the body bag when the *whoop* came rushing through the mountain air. Everyone immediately came to attention and froze in their stances. Slowly they began to observe the forest around them, looking for anything that might be looking back at them. There were no more *whoops*. As a matter of fact, there were no more sounds at all. The entire area had fallen silent; only a few rattles of the leaves could be heard as the breeze passed by them.

Elaine whispered, "They know we're here, Rob."

Rob whispered back, "You sure, Elaine? That sounded pretty far out the mountain."

Wilson responded, "I don't know, Rob, it's hard to tell how sounds are going to travel through this dense forest. We got Mr. Long. Let's get started back."

Whitney turned and faced Wilson. "Aaron's down there by himself."

Wilson spoke, "I know, but we got to go slow and methodically. We'll get Aaron on our way down the mountain. Harold, you lead the group, and I will bring up the rear... Rob and Elaine, you carry Mr. Long till we get to Aaron. He can help Rob till we get to the road, okay?"

Rob and Elaine picked up the bag with Elaine in front and Rob at the back of the bag. Whitney slid into formation between Elaine and Harold, and everyone turned to look at Wilson except Harold, who was intently guarding the 180 degrees in front of the party.

Wilson removed the fedora from his head and wiped the sweat from his eyebrows. After he firmly replaced the hat, he gave the command, "Okay, people. Let's go nice and easy."

The group traversed through the forest without a single word spoken. Harold continued to be vigilant in protecting the others from the front.

Wilson was walking a few steps behind the group, constantly taking two or three steps at a time; then, he would swing around and observe the woods behind them. When Wilson was confident that the rear was clear, he would turn and repeat the procedure.

Even though they were now walking downhill, it took even longer than the journey up the mountain. Everyone was on high alert. Just as Harold reached the transition of the mountain where it became steeper, the foul odor smacked him right in the face. He stopped and scanned the forest around them as the smell engulfed everyone in the search party.

Elaine now had an idea of just how close the creature was that made the whooping sound. She turned to Wilson and released her right hand from the bag. With her index finger, she pointed to her mouth and simply moved her lips, "Close."

Nobody else was looking in Wilson's direction when he nodded yes. The others were too busy scanning the forest or imagining the worst. Harold then focused on the spot where they left Aaron, but there was no sign of him. He maneuvered to his left to get a better angle at the area. He could see no sign of Aaron.

Harold turned to Wilson, who was cautiously searching the woods behind them, and whispered, "Aaron's gone."

Wilson spun around. "What?"

"Aaron's not where we left him."

Wilson said, "Everybody be careful... Get us down there, Harold."

Harold nodded, turned, and began to lead the group down the mountain.

***

The solemn silence of the forest was broken as the rock impacted the forest floor and began to tumble down the mountain. It crashed through the small limbs of the saplings between its collisions with the earth as it plummeted toward the old, abandoned road—which it would have made it to, had it not collided with the large tree that Jeff Sizemore was standing beside. Jeff was already assuming a crouching position while covering his head with his hands for protection. Brad Easton had raised his weapon to a firing position. He was moving the gun from left to right, searching for a target. The four below the road were well down the mountainside and did not hear the crashing sounds of the rock.

Next came the *whoop* either from the meadow or just on the other side of it, then came the grunt from up on the mountain above the road. All seven clearly heard both sounds. Immediately, Ronnie, Alicia, and Shelley crouched down and slid close to an old log lying on the floor of the forest. David held the weapon in a defensive position and was rotating his eyes between the hillside and the meadow. Probably just a minute had passed when the bellowing howl emerged from the head of the meadow. It chilled the seven people to the bone, and then as quickly as it had begun, the forest fell silent. Everybody remained frozen in their position until Brad took a quick glance to make sure he had Jeff and Joe still in view. Just as Brad was going to motion for the two of them to approach him, Jeff made his move. In the blink of an eye, Jeff bolted down the bank and began to run down the road toward the cabins.

Brad said, "No, Jeff!"

But it was too late; the fear had already taken hold, and Jeff wasn't stopping for love or money. He probably wasn't 50 yards down the road when Joe decided to follow him. Joe slid through the leaves on his rear end and rolled down the bank to the roadbed. As soon as he collided with the level dirt of the road, Joe sprang to his feet and began to chase Jeff in retreat. Brad was going to yell at both of the men but was interrupted by yet another howl coming from up on the mountainside. Brad tried to determine if the howl came from the same creature that grunted or if now there were more of them above him, looking down the mountain.

While everything was running rampart through Brad's brain, suddenly there came another *whoop* in or near the meadow. One more came from the head of the meadow, and then the area went silent once more. During all the commotion, Ronnie, Alicia, Shelley, and the body bag remained close to the fallen log. It was only after the area became silent again that Ronnie felt the sharp pain in his ankle. The apparent haste to seek cover had yielded Ronnie with a severely twisted ankle that was now shooting sharp pains through his leg. The three remained snugly against the damp bark of the log, trying to make themselves invisible to anything in the woods.

Finally, Shelley rose to her knees and placed her hands on the downed tree facing David and the meadow, but there was no sign of David. In fact, as she turned to look up at the old road, there was no sign of anyone. She slid back down to a sitting position. "Guys, I think we are alone," she said.

Ronnie whispered, "Where's David and what about the other three above us?"

Shelley answered, "I don't know... I don't see anyone."

Ronnie heavily sighed, "Great, here we go again. Plus, now I've got a bad ankle."

Alicia interjected, "What?"

"It's only twisted... I can walk, but I'm gonna be slow."

David was moving in a crawling manner to the edge of the tree line in order to get a better view of the meadow. The entire time, he was thinking, *If I can get a shot at one of these things, I'll be the first person to have definitive proof that these creatures do exist. Might just take a little glory from Wilson.* David smiled as he thought to himself how cool that would be. David was no longer thinking about protecting the others; it was all about self-gratification now. The other people still had Brad to look after them, he reasoned. There might not be a better opportunity than this. Slowly and methodically, he moved from one position to another, always keeping a keen eye on the grassy meadow. All David needed was for one of these creatures to slip up, and he would ultimately have his prize. The only setback was that David didn't know exactly what he was dealing with.

Brad was confused as to what his next move should be. He desperately wanted to make contact with the others below the road, but he realized that Joe and Jeff were his responsibility. Brad lowered himself to the ground to a sitting position. Slowly he used the heels of his boots to pull himself back down toward the road. He kept a close eye out to the left, to the right, and above him on the mountain. It was a painstakingly slow operation, but he felt it necessary for his own safety. Once at the bank dropping down to the road, he paused one more time to take a quick look around.

Confident that he was alone, Brad slid down the bank. Now he was totally exposed in the open space that was the old, abandoned road. Brad glanced up the road for just a second and then turned to look down the road. Already there was no sign of Jeff or Joe. He stepped to the side of the road, fully expecting to make visual contact with the four people who were searching down below. As he peered down the hill toward the meadow and the bay, there was not a single person in sight.

Things started to race through Brad's mind. Did one of the creatures get all four people down the mountain? Did everybody run like Jeff and Joe? If they did run, which direction did they go? Brad continued to scan the woods and cypher through all the things running through his mind.

Brad returned to the center of the road, where he took a quick scan of the area surrounding him. Ultimately, he decided his next move was to head for the cabins. At least he knew for sure that was the direction that Jeff and Joe were heading.

He had no idea of how close he actually was to the three people hiding behind the fallen log.

CHAPTER 14

Aaron was crashing through the woods like a madman. Nothing was racing through his mind but the thought of finding the old, abandoned road and getting back to the loading zone for the rafts. Fear had taken over every part of his body, and now he was concerned about nothing but his own self-preservation. His first objective came into view just as he grabbed a small sapling to remain in the upright position as he descended down the mountain.

Just ahead he spotted the exposed dirt of the old road, he could still smell the musky odor all around him with each gasp of air that he sucked in in his hasty retreat. Just as he was coming down the bank beside the road, Aaron lost his footing and crashed headfirst toward the ground. Luckily, he got his hands out in front of him just before impact. Aaron made a quick assessment of his physical wellbeing and dusted the dirt off his hands. In one seemingly choreographed motion, he came back to his feet and turned for the assault up the road. About three steps into his fearful flight, Aaron came to an abrupt halt.

Standing in the middle of the road approximately 50 yards ahead was a massive figure that appeared to be the largest man he had ever seen. Except this was no man blocking Aaron's exit; this thing was not like anything Aaron had ever laid eyes on. It was easily twice the size of himself, and in the moment of panic Aaron turned 180 degrees and began to run down the road as fast as he could—to where, he wasn't sure. Any place had to be better than the spot he emerged from the forest. The thought of finding a spot to turn down toward the shoreline raced through Aaron's mind with each and every impact of his boots on the surface of the road.

The group descending down the mountain finally reached the spot they had left Aaron at earlier. Everybody paused and slowly took a long look around. Then, Whitney asked, "Did he just take off alone, or did...?"

Harold was studying the forest floor below them. "Appears it was the first option, Whitney." Then, he turned to Wilson. "Looks like Aaron scooted a little way before grabbing a foothold and taking off down the mountain."

Wilson adjusted the fedora hat on his head. "Maybe the odor triggered him, or maybe the whooping sound drove him into the frenzy to retreat. He's probably heading back to the loading zone. All we can do now is to get ourselves back to the same spot."

Harold responded, "I agree. Everyone, go slow and watch your step."

Harold turned once again to face down the mountain and began to descend. Each of the individuals fell into his tracks as they began to traverse down the mountain. It was a slow, tedious process but necessary to ensure nobody got injured. The group did not need another person who required assistance.

Jeff was moving down the old road as if he was in the sprint of his life with a bleacher full of people chanting his name. Joe was trying to catch or at least keep pace with Jeff out in front of him. At every turn of the road, Joe could see that he might just be losing a step or two in his quest, but at least he had a visual of Jeff as he rounded each curve.

Suddenly, from above the two men emerged the deep, bellowing howl that seemed to vibrate the very ground they were running on. Next came the sound of something crashing through the leaves as it approached the road. Joe came to an immediate halt as he feared the worst. The rock that was rolling down the hillside passed between two large trees and crossed the road. As the two men stood there frozen in their tracks, the *whoop* could be clearly heard somewhere in the distance behind them. It didn't take Joe long to realize that the creatures had accomplished what they had set out to achieve. The group was now separated and having to fend for themselves. Joe wondered if Jeff was still running or if he'd stopped also.

Slowly, Joe began to take small steps to hopefully see if Jeff was standing up ahead around the curve. The forest had once again fallen silent. There was no movement on the ground or in the trees. As Joe moved around the curve, he stared down the vacant road to the next bend. There was no sign of Jeff; maybe he was indeed still running. As Joe continued to stare down the road, he noticed movement coming from around the curve ahead. After a moment of panic, he realized that Jeff wasn't still running but was now making his way back to him. Just as Jeff caught a glimpse of Joe, he stopped and gently waved.

Joe had his arm about halfway raised to return the gesture when the creature bolted from the road below. With one swipe of its mighty arm, the creature backhanded Joe directly in the middle of his chest. The blow knocked the wind out of Joe and sent him careening into the bank on the upper side of the road.

As soon as Jeff saw what was unfolding in front of him up the road, he wheeled around and once again began to sprint. He knew there was nothing he could do for Joe. At least in his mind, that's how he justified his return to the hasty retreat.

Joe Wilburn was struggling to get a breath when the creature slammed the massive foot into the middle of his back, pinning him to the ground. He fought feverishly to try and move in the dirt of the road, but it was no use. The pressure on his back had him pinned like trapped prey. Suddenly two more feet appeared on the road in front of Joe. As he stared at the feet directly in front of him, the first creature lifted its foot and released the pressure pinning him to the ground. Then, without warning, Joe felt a sudden rush of pain throughout his back and chest as the first creature slammed its foot into his back, this time with much more force. Just for a split-second, Joe felt his spine crush and the sensation of the bone fragments piercing his internal organs. Then, the world went dark for him, and his life ended. The two creatures studied Joe's body for signs of life, but there were none. Confident that this intruder was no longer a threat, the two creatures simply walked away and disappeared back into the forest.

***

Shelley, Ronnie, and Alicia were still hiding behind the fallen tree when they heard the bellowing howl from the mountainside down the road. Alicia snuggled against the tree as close as possible as the sound echoed all the way past the meadow. She closed her eyes as the *whoop* made its way through the trees and gently passed beyond them into the opening of the grassy area. Then, the forest fell silent again and the only sounds that any of the three could hear was the beating of their hearts along with the breaths they were taking in.

Shelley turned to Ronnie. "I think something must have happened down the road."

Ronnie sighed, "You may be right... I can't believe these people just left us out here."

"Maybe they are hiding just like we are," Alicia suggested.

Shelley responded, "Yeah, that's possible. But where did David go? He's nowhere to be seen. So much for protecting us."

Ronnie said, "I think we got Wilson and David figured out, but I was kinda hoping that Brad was on our side. At least for the protection part... you know."

Shelley raised slowly up on her knees. "Yep, I was hoping that, too. There's only one way to be sure if those guys are still up there. I'm going to take a look."

Alicia placed her hand on Shelley's elbow. "You're not going up there, are you?"

Shelley answered, "We've got to be sure that we're truly alone. Then we got to come up with a plan to get back to the loading zone for pickup. If nobody is still up there, then something may have very well happened going down the road to the cabins, and if it did... We need an alternate route for going back."

Alicia asked, "And just what are our options on that?"

Ronnie replied, "We'll be going down the shoreline just like last year."

Shelley nodded and smiled. "Just like old times, huh?"

Ronnie shook his head. "Yeah, just like old times."

Shelley winked at Alicia and began to move from the tree to start up the hillside. She moved as quietly as possible, careful not to make any sudden movements. After several minutes of maneuvering through the forest combined with pauses to survey her surroundings, Shelley finally reached the edge of the road. She wasn't totally convinced, but for the time being Ronnie and Alicia's eyes were the only ones focused on her. Shelley laid on her stomach and crawled to the edge of the road, then she peered in all directions in search of another human being. After just a brief time, she realized they were right; they were indeed alone and would have to make it back on their own.

After another quick glance around, Shelley slowly retreated back down the bank and began to make her way back to the fallen tree. About halfway down the hillside, she stopped as the *whoop* came from the other side of the meadow. Only a couple of seconds later, the three knocks were clearly audible from the head of the grassy clearing. Once again, the entire area fell deathly silent. After approximately a minute, Shelley continued down the hillside to rejoin Ronnie and Alicia. When she arrived there, Shelley knelt in exactly the same spot she occupied before she parted.

Alicia whispered, "So?"

Shelley tilted her head. "It's just as we figured... We are all alone."

Ronnie glanced down toward the bay. "We'll make our way down to the shoreline, and then we'll take our time going down the shore."

"Ronnie, can you walk on that ankle?" Alicia asked.

"I can limp on it, but you two may have to help me around some of the obstacles. That's our only choice."

Shelley looked all around. "He's right, Alicia. We don't know where any of the others are, and just like last year I don't believe we want to travel back down the road."

Ronnie looked at Shelley and smiled. "Well, at least I learned one thing from last year, Shelley."

"Yeah, what's that?" Shelley asked.

"I put a flashlight in my backpack... You know, just in case."

Shelley grinned. "That means we got two flashlights this year."

Alicia held up three fingers. "Nope. We got three lights, people."

Shelley glanced at Alicia. "That's good, because we are gonna need them. There's no way we are gonna be able to make it back by dark."

***

David had slowly made his way along the tree line that bordered the meadow, and now he was about halfway between the bay and the woods at the grassy expanse. He had heard the howl down the road and the *whoops* that encircled the area, but so far he had made no visual sighting of the creature. David eased into a spot just a few feet up the hillside where one large tree had fallen across a downed log to produce a V shape. This gave him a good view of the meadow to spot anything that attempted to travel across the grassy area. If something happened to move from behind him, David was positive he could hear it in the leaves. Surely he would be able to react in ample time to ward off any threat from above him. David sat perfectly still, only moving his eyes as he scanned the meadow. The tops of the tall grasses gently danced back and forth with the tiny breezes as they traveled across the meadow. *This is the spot*, he thought to himself. *The perfect place to wait out for the moment to bag one of these creatures.*

David thought of how cool it was going to be when he finally had proof that bigfoot, or this so-called Hairy Man, actually existed. His name would be mentioned in every bigfoot hunting show that aired on television. All of the podcast programs would throw his name out there for all to hear. David grinned a little as he sat there quietly. He would sit there until the opportunity presented itself, then take full advantage of the situation. All he had to do now was wait—wait for the moment.

Harold was the first one of the group coming down the mountain to spot the old road. He took a couple more steps before coming to a stop beside a large pine tree. Harold held out his arm to signal the others to halt. He searched in both directions of the abandoned road for any movement but saw nothing. Next, Harold motioned for the group to stay put as he began to travel the last few steps to the road. Once he was standing directly on the roadbed, Harold took another look in both directions, but all was clear. He then looked down to the area between the trees and the road itself. It was clear that a disturbance had occurred in the leaves and the dirt; it appeared that something had slid on the surrounding ground. The next thing he noticed was the large footprint adjacent to the slide marks, a large humanoid print that was much larger than the boots he wore. As Harold took another look up the road, he noticed the spot that gave the appearance of someone changing directions in a really big hurry.

Harold turned to the others and placed his index finger against his lips, then he motioned for everybody to make their way to the road. Once the group, along with Mr. Long, were assembled on the road, Harold looked at Wilson and whispered, "I don't think Aaron is headed for the landing zone."

Rob spoke next, "Surely he didn't take a wrong turn."

Harold answered, "I don't think so... It looks like he fell coming out of the trees. See the spot where his hands slid in the dirt. Next, he came to his feet and started up the road, but for some reason he reversed directions and began going down the road."

Elaine asked, "Why would he do that? Surely he didn't forget which way we came, did he?"

Harold shook his head, "No, I think he saw something that made him change directions. Look at that footprint in the soil where he slid."

Wilson took a couple of steps and knelt on one knee to study the print. "My gosh... That's a massive print. You can clearly see the impression each toe made, and if Aaron did see this thing, one can only imagine what went through his mind."

Harold turned to Elaine. "Down the road, that's where the old home-stead is, right?"

Elaine answered, "Yes."

"How far?"

Elaine looked down the road and then back at Harold. "I have no idea, but if I was guessing... We are close to being halfway between the cabins and the homestead."

Wilson chimed in next, "We don't have time to go and search for Aaron as a group. It'll be dark before we can get back anywhere close to the landing area."

Harold said, "I agree. You take the group back, and I'll go and look for Aaron. As soon as these people are on the raft, you start back down the road to me Wilson, but don't call on the radio because I won't have mine on. I don't want these things to hear us talking and get the drop on us, okay?"

Wilson said, "I'll be back as soon as possible. Keep a sharp eye out, and if you have to shoot, make sure of your target."

Harold smiled. "I promise not to shoot you, Wilson."

Wilson grinned back at Harold. "Thanks, buddy. I'll show you the same courtesy."

Harold turned and started moving down the road. Wilson began to lead the others up the road toward the cabins. Rob now assumed the position at the rear of the group, while Wilson had the lead. Whitney placed her hand on the body bag beside Elaine's to assist with Mr. Long.

CHAPTER 15

Back on the ship, Captain Frank was standing on the deck at the bow of the boat. He was staring intently at the area around the cabins watching for any sign of the search parties. Periodically, he would lift the binoculars to his eyes to take a closer look at the old, abandoned road that stretched behind the cabins in both directions, but so far the captain had no luck in spotting any of the team members. Captain Frank had clearly heard the bellowing howl that emerged from the forest toward the meadow, and he had taken note of the deer grazing above the cabins darting into the trees when the howl made its way down to the cabins.

The captain thought to himself how everything at the port respected the creatures that walked these woods. Perhaps he was right after all—coming back to this place was indeed a bad idea. As the minutes continued to tick away after the vocalization, Captain Frank became more and more concerned for the safety of the others. Unfortunately, all he could do now was wait and watch. This was not a feeling that the captain was the least bit comfortable with.

***

Jeff Sizemore had been running for what seemed like an eternity, each bend in the road only welcoming another view of the same thing. With each corner he rounded, there was just another section of the exposed dirt of the road with the next curve ahead, and none of it he clearly remembered. Jeff's mind was beginning to play games in his head. At times, he imagined that possibly he had mistakenly taken a wrong turn in his hasty retreat. Almost as quickly as his mind began to drift, Jeff would snap back to reality and realize there had been no turns on the hike up. Only game trails intersected the road as they crisscrossed from side to side. But Jeff was still wondering why it was taking so long to reach the clearing of the cabins. Suddenly he regretted not paying better attention as the group made their way up the old road.

Just as Jeff rounded the next curve, he spotted a familiar site up ahead: the shelter that the creature constructed for Shelley and Ronnie to protect them from the elements. As Jeff approached the makeshift shelter, he came to a halt. Slowly he knelt down on both knees and placed his right hand on his side. He could not remember running this hard since he was a child, and Jeff definitely couldn't ever remember being this afraid. After several minutes of trying to recover from what he had just experienced, Jeff decided to make another run to try and reach the clearing. Just as Jeff placed his left hand firmly onto the dirt to assist in coming back to his feet, he spotted something ahead. Jeff caught a glimpse of something crossing the road.

There was no mistaking what the large figure was. He paused for several seconds, trying to determine what his next move would be. In his mind, Jeff could not conclude if the creature had continued down the mountainside, or maybe it was just hiding on the lower side of the road waiting to ambush another victim. Quite possibly the same method used to attack Joe. Jeff started to scan the woods above him for an escape route. Finally, he decided his best option was to climb up the mountain and try to sneak out of the forest above the road. After a few more minutes of studying his surroundings, Jeff came to his feet and as quietly as possible began to ascend up the hillside.

***

Bodyguard Brad was methodically placing one foot in front of the other as he slowly traversed back down the road. It was a painstakingly slow process, but he was intent on having a clear picture of everything going on around him. Brad knew for certain they were not alone in these woods; he just wasn't sure of how many of these creatures were in the woods with them. Finally, the limp figure came into view just ahead on the road, and right away Brad knew that one of the men running down the road was not gonna make it to the landing zone. While keeping a watchful eye out, Brad made his way to the body. Once he got close, Brad realized it was Joe Wilburn from the network by the clothes he wore. The man was lying face down in the dirt with a small pool of blood oozing onto the soil from both sides of his chest underneath the body.

Brad took special notice of the large compression spot in the middle of Joe's back. He could only imagine the force it took to inflict this kind of injury. Brad slowly lifted his head and scanned the woods around him. Even though he saw nothing, Brad had the uneasy feeling that he was being watched. As he studied the area, Brad contemplated taking Joe with him but knew he would be unable to defend himself with the extra burden. Ultimately, he decided to leave Joe and continue down the road. Brad hoped he still had time to locate Jeff, maybe before he met the same fate.

***

Aaron bolted through the opening at the edge of the forest and suddenly found himself in the clearing that held the old homestead. He paused for a moment and began running down the path that led to the old structures. Initially, his plan was to bypass the old house and continue to the shoreline. Aaron thought if he could make it to the shoreline, he could possibly signal the boat, and the crew could rescue him. About 20 yards from the old homestead, Aaron heard several grunts coming from somewhere in the trees below the house. Next came the high-pitched scream from the mountainside above the clearing that ran cold chills through Aaron's entire body.

The next step Aaron turned to take refuge in the old house, a large deer came bolting between the house and the old toolshed adjacent to it. Aaron made another quick adjustment in his effort to avoid a collision with the animal and lost his footing. The impact with the ground produced a sharp shooting pain in his left shoulder. Aaron continued to crawl to the house on both knees and one arm until he reached the spot where the front door once stood. As quickly as possible, he slid into the opening and propped himself against the inner wall. Now, Aaron's brain was racing at a frantic rate. Where exactly were these things, and had they actually seen him or not? Maybe he had hidden just in time, and perhaps these vocalizations were just normal happenings that occurred every day.

Aaron decided to take a few minutes to see if things might possibly calm down, and slowly his situation began to sink into his mind. There was a creature between him and the landing zone. Something was above him on the mountain, and the grunting sounds came from between him and the shoreline. The only open area was down the road, but there was no explanation of what was below the old homestead; nobody traveled beyond this point last year.

Next came the distinct sound of an object impacting the roof of the home. It bounced a couple of times and slowly rolled down the old wooden shingles. Aaron's heart began to beat faster, and suddenly a second object impacted the outside of the wall Aaron was leaning against.

Now, Aaron was completely sure the creatures knew exactly where he was. He came to his feet and made his way to where the old fireplace stood. A set of fireplace utensils still stood in their stand on the hearth, and Aaron spotted the pointed fire poker. It was the only weapon that Aaron could find at the moment. As he grabbed the tool and held it firmly in his right hand, the pain in the opposite shoulder seemed to completely disappear. Now fear was running through every inch of his body. Just as Aaron caught a glimpse of the old skull lying on the floor of the old home, he heard something moving in the grass outside. Then, he saw something move by one of the old windows that somehow had withstood the test of time. He heard grunts coming from the area outside that seemed to encircle the entire house. Aaron realized he was now surrounded.

He had to somehow stand his ground. First he yelled for the whatever was outside to go away and then banged the rocks of the fireplace with the poker. For the moment, Aaron believed his tactic might have done the trick as he listened for any sounds coming from outside. He made his way over to the window as he held the poker tightly in his hand for defense and stopped about a foot from the glass and closely watched for any movement in the tall grass. Next, Aaron heard a noise of something coming across the floor of the old home and turned just in time to see the small rock collide with the broken arm of an old chair. The next sound Aaron heard was the shattering glass of the window as the massive arm reached in and grabbed Aaron by the throat. In one single movement, Aaron's feet left the floor, and his body was ripped through the spot the window once occupied. The poker slammed into the window trim and tore from his hand.

Aaron's feet never touched the ground outside surrounding the homestead before his body changed directions and his head was slammed into the outside wall of the house. Aaron was just barely conscious enough to realize his body was flying through the air like a ragdoll tossed in the backyard of a neighborhood house. The impact of Aaron's head rendered him into darkness, which turned out to be a blessing for him. The first creature that approached him tightly gripped its large hand around Aaron's throat and began to squeeze. Just as the second creature grabbed Aaron's arm, his neck began to crush, and the blood started to ooze from the ruptured flesh.

Aaron was now totally oblivious as to what was taking place. In the tug of war that was now ensuing, the second creature ripped Aaron's arm from his lifeless body. It turned and hurled the appendage toward the bay. The first creature still had a firm grip on the limp figure that once was a man, and after a brief moment the creature tossed Aaron's body into the tall grass that bordered the homestead.

All the beasts that were at the old home simply disappeared back into the forest.

***

Harold never heard the grunts below the house, but the high-pitched scream up on the mountain stopped him dead in his tracks. He had never heard anything like that before. A mountain lion made sounds similar to the scream, but Harold knew this was no big cat hollering up on the mountain. The forest around him was now eerily quiet; there were no sounds or movement of any kind. Harold glanced at the trees that surrounded him on the road and noticed there was not even a small bird in sight. *What kind of a creature shuts the entire forest down?* he thought. After a minute, Harold started moving once again down the road to the homestead, taking small easy steps and keeping a watchful eye on the forest that bordered the road. Harold kept his weapon in a ready-to-fire position at all times while he moved along. It seemed to take forever, but finally in front of Harold was the opening to the homestead. The late afternoon sun rays were beaming from the open air onto the old, abandoned road. Harold felt a sigh of relief from the dimly lit forest as he approached the clearing.

Harold eased to the edge of the clearing on the upper side of the road and situated himself against a large tree, pausing for several minutes as he studied the clearing. As far as he could tell, the area around the homestead was void of any danger at the moment. Harold wondered if Aaron had indeed taken shelter in one of the structures below him. He saw no movement whatsoever in or around the buildings in the middle of the clearing, but if Aaron was truly down there he was probably hiding and afraid to move, he thought. Harold hoped the scream above the homestead would possibly convince Aaron to stay close or maybe to hide in one of these structures.

Even though the open area gave Harold a better view of things, he knew that if something else was watching it would give it a better view of him as he approached the buildings. In his mind, Harold knew he had to go and search the house. Hopefully, he could locate Aaron and return him safely to the boat. After a few more minutes of scanning, Harold stepped out from behind the tree, and almost instantly he was walking in the open expanse that once was roamed by the people who lived here.

***

Ronnie was sitting in the leaves with his back against the fallen tree. He exhaled a large breath and said, "We need to get started back, girls. It's gonna be a slow trip with this ankle."

Shelley looked around through the woods and then turned to Alicia. "Ronnie's right. Let's move straight down the woods to the shoreline. Try to be as quiet as possible."

Alicia took hold of Ronnie's elbow, and she whispered, "Come on, honey."

With the help of Alicia, Ronnie came to his feet and slowly applied a little pressure to the injured foot. He tested his ability to walk and then looked at both of the women. "I think if we go slow, I may be able to hobble along," he said. "It's just going to take me a little longer."

Shelley smiled. "Well... Since you did most of the work last year going down the shoreline, the least that Alicia and I can do is assist you this time."

Ronnie said, "I appreciate it, girls... Let's get to the shoreline while the tide is still low."

Alicia moved to Ronnie's side, and Shelley picked up the body bag containing the bone they had recovered. Shelley placed the bag over her shoulder and started to move around the others to lead the way. After taking a couple of steps, she paused and lowered the bag to the ground. Next, Shelley removed her backpack and unzipped it to expose the main compartment. As she lowered herself down on one knee, Shelley removed the pistol that Captain Frank had graciously supplied and gently placed it on the leaves. Ronnie and Alicia remained silent as Shelley rummaged through the pack. Once she found what she was looking for, Shelley looked up at the two of them.

Shelley grinned and said, "Sorry... Just remembered that I brought more than just a flashlight." She twisted the cap of the small bottle and handed Ronnie two ibuprofen tablets. "These might help a little."

Alicia then handed her water bottle to Ronnie, and he popped the tablets into his mouth and washed them down with a large gulp of water. Alicia replaced her water bottle in her backpack holder. Shelley zipped her pack and hoisted it onto her back. After adjusting the backpack, Shelley once again grabbed the black body bag and slung it over her shoulder. With her free hand, she gripped the pistol and rose to her feet so they could start down the mountain.

Luckily, the slope down the hillside from their position at the fallen log was a steady and gradual descent. There were the normal fallen trees and stumps to navigate around, but at least the ground under their feet did not present a lot of problems. Every now and then, a little too much pressure on Ronnie's foot in just the right direction would cause him to wince, and the rest of his body would drop to favor the foot, but Alicia would add the extra support to help him. Shelley was constantly scanning the forest looking for any danger that might confront them. Periodically she would glance at the pistol she held tightly in her hand to reassure herself of the location of the safety mechanism in case she needed to switch it to the fire position at a moment's notice.

It had taken much longer than any of the three ever imagined making their way down the hillside, but finally they could see the water of the bay and the exposed shoreline that surrounded it. As they reached the edge of the trees, Ronnie, with the help of Alicia, sat on his rear end and slid the last few feet until the seat of his britches met the semi-sandy soil of the shore. Alicia and Shelley followed suit until all three were sitting on their bottoms, staring at the peaceful waters of the bay.

CHAPTER 16

Captain Frank was about to remove the flask from his jacket when he spotted movement on the old, abandoned road just to the left of the cabins. Almost instantly he lifted the binoculars to his eyes for a closer look. Within a matter of seconds, he saw the group searching for Mr. Long emerging from the forest. As each person cleared the trees, the captain counted. By the time the group started down the path to the loading zone, Captain Frank knew the group was two people short. The captain hurriedly walked to the ship's door and banged on the side of the boat with his fist. A young crew member opened the door and looked at the captain.

Captain Frank ordered the young crewman to get the raft ready and head to the shore for pickup. Immediately, the crewman started yelling commands inside the ship, and within no time at all the ship came to life. People were scurrying on the ship's deck and traversing the steps down to the landing platform to ready the raft. Every person had a specific job to do, and they were performing their duties with perfection. The captain once again turned to view the search party to try and figure out what two people were missing. The group was probably halfway down the path when the captain heard the outboard motor of the raft come to life. Soon, the crew were guiding the raft to the landing zone on the shore. Just as the group arrived, the raft slid onto the sandy shore.

The young man at the front of the raft stretched forth his hand to take the body bag, and Mr. Long was the first to board the raft. Next was Whitney and Elaine. Rob was the last of the group to slide into the small craft. Wilson leaned his rifle against a small tree, planted his feet in the soil, and grunted as he pushed the raft off the sandy area. Wilson quickly regained his composure, turned to retrieve the firearm, then began to make his way bay up the trail to the cabins.

The young lad reversed the outboard motor on the raft and swung it around until it was aimed at the ship in the bay. Then, he switched the lever on the engine and twisted the throttle. Whitney leaned against the side of the raft and exhaled a large breath. For the first time since she stepped on the shore that morning, Whitney felt safe. In short order, the driver of the raft positioned it against the edge of the platform of the ship. The crew member at the front leaped onto the platform and secured the vessel. One by one, the search party was assisted onto the ship by the crew. Captain Frank was standing on the bottom step with his right hand firmly gripping the handrail.

When Rob made eye contact with Frank, the captain asked, "What happened, where are the others?"

Rob answered, "Aaron couldn't make it all the way up the mountain to Mr. Long. Once we recovered the remains and started back down the mountain, Aaron wasn't at the spot we left him."

Captain Frank took a quick look around at everybody on the landing. "He never came up the road. I've been watching around the cabins."

Elaine shook her head. "It appears he may have started this way and then changed his mind. Harold went toward the old homestead to look for him... Wilson is heading back that way to assist Harold."

Captain Frank looked out over the bay. "It's already getting late in the afternoon. They're not gonna make it back before dark."

Rob responded, "No... Any word from the other group?"

The captain answered, "Haven't heard a word."

Elaine turned to look toward the grassy meadow. "Let's get Mr. Long with the others, then maybe we can call the others on the radio."

Captain Frank sighed, "We can try, but there hasn't been any chatter on the radios all day. I heard the howl from the direction of the meadow and the scream from the mountainside above the homestead. I really doubt if any of the radio devices are switched on. The men are probably trying to stay as quiet as possible. I know that is exactly what I would be doing."

The two young crewmen picked up the body bag and began to climb the steps to the ships deck, and the others fell into line and followed the young men. Once they reached the top of the steps, the crew took a left as they escorted Mr. Long to the holding room for the remains. The rest of the people continued to the bow of the ship and positioned themselves to observe the area around the cabins from a year ago.

Captain Frank patted Rob on the shoulder and said, "You guys keep lookout. I'm gonna try and reach the others."

Everyone continued to stare intently at the cabin area, hoping to catch a glimpse of someone returning to the boat. Wilson had already disappeared into the trees heading back down the road, and there was no sign of anyone anywhere. After just a couple of minutes, the captain emerged from the ships door and closed it behind him. After making his way to the group, he simply shook his head. "Just as I figured... They must have their radios off. No response."

Everybody shifted to look back at the clearing, and Whitney spoke, "If they don't make it soon, they will be caught out there in the darkness."

Captain Frank leaned onto the railing. "And that is what concerns me."

Elaine asked, "What about the second group? We know their direction. Should we go look for them?"

The captain answered, "There's no way any of us can make it up there before dark now, so our only option is to stay right here on the boat. We can keep an eye out from the deck of the ship. If anyone needs our assistance, they can signal, and we can go straight to them and pick them up."

Rob was the next to speak, "As bad as I hate to admit it... The captain is right. We watch for anyone that may need our help."

Captain Frank added, "If we spot anything, even after dark, we can take the raft right to them and pick them up."

Everybody agreed. Even Elaine nodded her head, even though it was kind of reluctantly. But she knew in her mind that it was the only logical thing to do.

***

Jeff Sizemore had no earthly idea of where he was at. Every now and then, he could catch a small glimpse of the water in the bay through a gap in the canopy of the trees. But for several minutes now, the underbrush of the forest had become so thick he could not see the old road below him. Periodically, Jeff would stop to listen for any noise close by. He wasn't sure if the silence was a good thing or not. All Jeff could think was that somehow he needed to intersect the clearing of the cabins before dark. The sun had already begun to pass over the edge of the mountain peaks that surrounded the bay, and he knew there was only a short window of time before darkness would fill the forest. Suddenly, Jeff heard something rustling in the leaves somewhere above him, and in his mind he had no definitive answer for what it exactly was. As Jeff stood very still staring up the mountainside, he could feel every pounding beat of his heart as it pushed the blood through- out his entire body. Then from below came the sound of what Jeff imagined a small tree being shaken violently would sound like. The two sounds would alternate with each other, then there would be a few seconds of quietness, then the sounds would start again, breaking the silence of the forest. Fear was beginning to take over Jeff's entire body until finally he exploded in a mad dash through the forest toward the cabins.

Now, Jeff was not the least bit concerned with concealing his position as he crashed through the underbrush of the mountain. He barreled out the mountainside, knocking small saplings to the left and to the right in his pursuit of the clearing. Now Jeff could hear what sounded like grunts or growls below him keeping pace as he ran out the hillside. He heard nothing from above because of the noise Jeff was generating as he made his hasty escape. The race was on, and Jeff knew he was running for his life. He almost wanted to scream, but there wasn't time or efficient air in his lungs to produce the sound.

Just as Jeff heard the whooping sound coming down from above, he caught the toe of his boot on something hidden beneath the leaves, and in the next instant Jeff was tumbling on the forest floor. He quickly crawled next to a large tree and placed his back against it. Jeff was frantically sucking in air, trying to replenish his body. Quietness now engulfed the forest around him as he scanned the woods for any danger. For an instant, Jeff thought he might just pull this off. He placed his hand on the moist soil of the hillside and slowly raised himself until he was leaning against the large tree. Jeff was constantly blinking his eyes, trying to clear away the sweat rolling off his forehead in an effort to see somewhat clearly. Just as he got a split second of clear vision, Jeff spotted just exactly what was making the tree-shaking sounds below him. He glanced out in front of him and could see that just ahead was the clearing of the cabins. Jeff decided now was the time to bolt for the opening.

Just as Jeff pushed away from the tree to make his run for the clearing, the massive muscular arm reached from around the tree. The hand clinched tightly on the clothing at his chest. The man did his best to scream, but there was no sound that emerged from his mouth. Jeff was hurled down the mountain like a small stuffed animal. He impacted the ground with a loud thud and rolled down the mountainside, grabbing at anything and everything. He only came to a stop because of the collision with a stump that was in his path.

Jeff immediately came to his feet, turned to the clearing, and started to run. But standing between him and the edge of the grassy area was the creature that had been keeping pace from below him. With one mighty motion, the creature slammed its fist into Jeff's chest, sending the fragments of his sternum deep into the heart muscle. Jeff's heart may have only beat one or two times after the crushing blow. The sheer force of the punch not only splintered his sternum, but also it tore the aorta artery away from the heart itself.

The creature from above only observed the activity taking place below it. The creature that delivered the blow picked up Jeff's body and slammed it into the forest floor several times. There was a moment of silence in the woods until both creatures were confident that Jeff was indeed dead, then the one that delivered the fatal blow arched its back and released the bellowing howl. This time, all that was on the mountainside and those standing on the bow of the boat clearly heard the roar. Those at the ship stared intently at the spot it originated from.

***

Shelley, Ronnie, and Alicia were still sitting on the sandy shoreline when the howl came rushing down the mountain to them. All three swiveled their heads in the direction of the sound as it made its way by them to the head of the bay. Alicia turned to Ronnie and said, "What was that all about?"

Ronnie only shifted his eyes to Alicia as he answered, "Not a hundred percent sure, but I don't think it was a warning sound to anyone."

Shelley had never taken her eyes off of the mountain. "Neither do I... I think something bad just happened."

Alicia began, "Do you think one of the others...?"

Shelley turned to face Alicia and Ronnie. "By now, we all know these things are here...even the new ones to the port. There's no doubt that they aren't trying to hide or disguise themselves from us. That almost sounded like a boastful gesture for a job well done."

Alicia looked out over the bay. "So, you think that someone just..."

Ronnie placed his hand on Alicia's wrist. "I think that is exactly what just happened. Unfortunately, we are all separated now, and we have to manage our own way back. Somehow we got to get close enough to try and signal the ship. I'm afraid it's gonna be a slow process, though. This ankle is going to slow us down."

Alicia placed her hand on Ronnie's pant leg and raised the material. "Ronnie, that ankle is really starting to swell, and there's a knot right above your boot."

Shelley shifted to take a look. "That might be more than just a sprain, ole boy."

Ronnie remarked, "Yeah... I could feel it coming down the mountain. I'll do the best I can."

Shelley smiled at Ronnie and said, "I have no doubt about that. I've ventured down this shoreline with you before."

Ronnie sighed, "Well, girls... We better get started."

Alicia was the first to come to her feet, and Ronnie stretched forth his hand to her. He let out a moan as Alicia helped him to his feet, and he placed a little pressure on the damaged ankle. Ronnie looked at Shelley and said, "This may be a little tougher than I thought."

Shelley picked up the body bag. "Alicia and I will take turns helping you down the shore. All we gotta do is get close enough to signal the ship. I'm pretty sure that the people on the boat will be watching... Let's go nice and easy."

Alicia placed Ronnie's arm over her shoulder, and the three of them began to make their way down the shore. Every few feet they would have to pause for Ronnie to rest and catch his breath. This appeared to be the process they would continue to deal with for quite some time. At least for now, there were no noises that any of them heard as they moved along.

***

David Felder was still tucked into his position when the howl came rushing through the trees. At first, his body jerked, and then he heard the sound echoing in the hills beyond the grassy meadow that lay in front of him. For a split second, the howl caught David off guard just enough to move his eyes from the spot on the far side of the meadow he had been focused on. Now when he looked back, the dark spot on the edge of the grass beside the tree line was gone. In David's mind, he realized that indeed there had been something there. All he had to do was locate whatever that was again, and the glory would be all his.

Suddenly, there were three distinct knocks from the head of the meadow. David slowly positioned his eyes to focus on that area as he firmly held the rifle against his lap. The view at the head of the meadow was growing darker by the minute as dusk began to creep into the port, and David eased his right hand down and unzipped his backpack lying next to him. He removed the night vision goggles and placed them on the ground next to him. He smiled as he thought to himself, *These creatures aren't the only ones who can see in the dark.*

CHAPTER 17

After a short span of easing down through the clearing in a crouched position, Harold was finally standing beside the old homestead. He took a brief moment to survey the area and listen for any sign that Aaron might be inside. He noticed that the sun had disappeared over the mountain top, and dusk was beginning to invade the area. Soon, darkness would engulf the entire port, but Harold found comfort in knowing he had eyes in the dark. Slowly, Harold inched to where the door of the homestead once stood and peered into the house. As he entered the building, Harold remained vigilant in scoping out every single inch that lay in front of him.

Harold was shocked at how the inside of the home remained relatively intact after all these years. There was still evidence of everyday supplies scattered in various spots around the house. Suddenly, there was the sound of movement coming from the corner of the one-room house. Harold wheeled in that direction and raised the firearm to greet whatever it was. A small chipmunk darted across a broken chair leg, hopped onto the hearth of the fireplace, and scurried to an opening in the wall to the outside of the old home. Harold lowered the firearm back down to his waist and exhaled a large sigh of relief.

Next, he noticed an oddity at the hearth as he stared at the fireplace utensils that were still neatly standing in their rack. One of the utensils was missing. To himself, Harold quietly wondered why all but one was still in their rightful place. He moved to the fireplace as stealthily as he could while keeping an eye on the rest of the room. Just a few feet away, Harold spotted the jawbone discovered from the previous year, and after he studied it for a few seconds he recognized the item to be that of a human being. Harold scanned the entire floor of the homestead, and the skull that Mark had mentioned in his report came into view. Right away, he noticed that the injuries to the skull were quite similar to those of Mr. Long when they found his remains.

Once Harold's eyes began to look around the cabin again, he noticed the missing fireplace utensil lying next to the broken window, and slowly he made his way to the window and fireplace poker. It was hard to determine when the glass had broken, but Harold noticed a fresh spot on the window trim where something had impacted the wood. Next was the bright red substance still clinging to a broken piece of glass, holding onto its spot in the wooden frame. Harold released his finger from the trigger of the gun and touched the substance with his index finger. Most of the blood had already dried, except for one small spot that smeared across the glass as Harold touched it. Now he realized why the fire poker had been removed from the stand. Aaron was trying to defend himself, probably from the same thing that the two individuals whose bones were on the floor had encountered.

Harold slowly walked back to the door of the homestead and paused for just a second as he studied the area outside the old home. He could see nothing, but his many years of being outdoors in the wild told him that there was something hidden somewhere watching his every move. He knew that these things were master hunters and were really efficient at singling out their prey for the attack. The thoughts continued to race through Harold's mind as his eyes moved in all directions, trying to grab a glimpse of whatever he knew was watching. These creatures had gotten the drop on Mr. Long, who was probably more of an outdoorsman than any of them, except for possibly Wilson. Mr. Long had weapons, night vision, and all the skills to survive just about anywhere.

But Mr. Long was still hunted down here at the port. Bill had a weapon. Tim was in the safety of the cabin with a firearm in hand, and both of them were now dead. Yet the creatures allowed some to survive. Perhaps Elaine's explanation of the compassion part was correct. It just didn't seem that it could be that simple to Harold. Anyway, it didn't really matter at the moment; Harold needed to find Aaron before darkness overtook the area. Harold knew where to start his search—outside the broken window. He stepped outside and made his way to the side of the homestead where Aaron met his fate.

**

Brad Easton came around one of the many curves of the road and spotted something just ahead on the upper side of the road. It was now dark enough that Brad was having difficulty not only seeing clearly in the forest but also in the openness of the old roadbed. After observing no movement of the object, Brad lowered to one knee and removed his backpack, and after finding the night vision goggles he focused on the dark spot in the road. It was now evident that Brad was looking at the shelter structure constructed for Ronnie and Shelley a year ago. After taking a deep breath, Brad came to his feet and approached the crude shelter. As he studied the woven trees that supported the pine limbs covering the ground, Brad noticed fresh marks in the soil of the road. Something or someone had been there just ahead of him. Brad scanned to his right and noticed where the leaves had been disturbed going up the bank into the forest. There in the dirt were fresh boot prints going up the bank and disappearing in the leaves of the mountainside.

Now, Brad had a pretty good idea what the last howl coming from the mountainside above the road was all about. He simply dropped his head when he came to grips with the fact that Jeff had more than likely met his demise on the side of the mountain just a little while earlier. For a moment, Brad became enraged at the thought of the two men running away. If only they hadn't let the panic take control, they could very well still be alive right now. As Brad looked down the road, he determined that in just a few more minutes it would be completely dark and impossible to find Jeff. The only thing to do was get to the landing zone, and maybe tomorrow they could return to search for Jeff.

***

As Wilson eased down the road, an uneasy feeling began to overtake him. He knew that if something was hunting ole Wilson, it would have the advantage as long as he was moving. Now it was relatively dark in the forest, and any animal could easily attack from anywhere in the trees at any time. Wilson had no idea of the whereabouts of Harold or Aaron. For all practical purposes, he didn't even know if they were still alive. Quite possibly, Harold had found Aaron, and they had taken an alternate way back to the boat. Wilson found a spot where he could silently enter into the woods and take refuge. Once he was several feet away from the road, Wilson took a minute to survey the area. He found the perfect spot to hide and watch the road.

If one of these things came walking by, it would be his turn to have the advantage. Wilson settled into his newfound hiding area to begin the nights hunt. There was a fallen log resting against a tree with a scrub bush placed just perfectly in front of him to conceal his presence. After clearing the leaves, Wilson snuggled into the spot and placed the rifle across his lap, then he began to observe all around him with the night vision goggles.

***

David Felder had been watching the grassy meadow from the confines of his hiding spot for quite some time, trying his best to get another glimpse of whatever the dark spot was that disappeared earlier from across the meadow. Ever since the howl from down the mountain just before dark, David had heard no other sounds. There had been no tree knocks or *whoops* from anywhere around him. David was beginning to wonder if he had chosen the correct spot for his hunt tonight. Then came the single *whoop* from across the meadow. The sound was not very loud, but it was clear enough for David to identify it as not being an owl's call. This was definitely one of the creatures, and David could feel the adrenalin start to run through his veins. Through the night vision goggles, David saw something leave the tree line and enter the tall grass. Slowly he laid the goggles to his side and readied the rifle. Now, David was watching the field through the night vision scope of the rifle, watching and waiting for this thing to show itself again. For the next minute, all David could capture in the scope was the occasional movement of the grass as something made its way down the meadow.

David had started to believe that whatever he was observing might be one of the many bears of the area. If it was one of these so-called Hairy Men and it was on two feet, he could surely see the creature. Then, three knocks at the head of the meadow broke the silence of the darkness. This was followed by a *whoop* from behind David's position. As he recovered from the response of hearing these sounds, David turned to take another look at the spot where he last seen the grass moving. Nearly halfway through the turning motion of his head and the rifle, David spotted something standing at the edge of the creek that flowed to the bay. Almost as quickly as David spotted the figure, it disappeared into either the creek or the grass, but he was sure the creature was standing on two feet.

David's heart began to beat faster and faster as he realized he was closer to taking his shot, only he hadn't figured out yet who was the hunter and who was the hunted. As a matter of fact, it hadn't dawned on David what exactly was happening. David was being played directly into the creatures' hands. Then came the *whoop* from the meadow between David and the bay, then another from the side of the creek facing him. Next was the loud grunt from behind his position and the bellowing howl from the head of the meadow. Things were happening faster than David was able to deal with. Now, his head appeared to be on a swivel chasing all the activity around him. The crashing in the leaves behind David alarmed him to raise upon his knees and take aim up the hillside. He barely reached the position to fire the weapon when the creature swung its mighty arm and struck David on the side of the head. As his body rotated toward the ground, the rifle aimlessly fired into the now star-filled sky. The sound of the gun expelling the bullet shattered the silence of the port as it echoed around the entire bay.

David was still tumbling down the hill when the creature he first spotted moving through the grass slammed its foot into his stomach. For just an instant, David realized that what had taken place was a well-planned attack, and he had been the hunted, not the hunter. The pain in David's stomach was excruciating as the ruptured organs began to spew blood internally in his body. The next thing that David realized was he had been picked up and was now being violently swung from side to side. David's body was impacting everything that was in the path of the creature's swing. Finally, the fatal blow came as David's head collided with the large tree and his skull gave way with the force of the collision.

The creature merely dropped the limp body onto the forest floor and released a bloodcurdling scream that traveled throughout the entire area.

***

Ronnie, Shelley, and Alicia had just taken another break in their journey down the shoreline. The pain in Ronnie's ankle was becoming almost unbearable. Each time his foot touched the ground, there were sharp pains that traveled all the way up his leg. He could feel that the ankle was not the only problem facing him. Ronnie hadn't told the girls yet, but he had started to run a fever a short time ago.

First, the gunshot shattered the silence around them, and then shortly after came the scream that pierced the night air. Each of them could feel the sensation of the goosebumps crawling up the back of their necks. Shelley was sitting on a large rock with her hands on her knees, and Ronnie and Alicia were resting directly on the soil of the shore with their backs against a piece of driftwood. Shelley slowly slid down the side of the rock until her rear end was firmly planted on the dirt and her back was against the rock. All were trying to muffle their breaths as they listened for any more activity around them.

After a couple of seconds, Alicia turned to Shelley and asked, "Was that scream one of us or one of them?"

Shelley was still staring in the direction of the meadow. "Them."

Ronnie arched his back and leaned his head back a little. "Had to be one of the bodyguards... David would be my guess."

"Yeah, mine too," Shelley said.

The conversation quickly came to a halt as the small branch snapped in the woods above them. Next was the sound of something taking a couple of steps in the leaves. Through what little light there was from the open bay around them, Ronnie could see Alicia focused on him. "It's gonna be okay," he said. "Do not shine your flashlight at anything but the ground, Alicia. No matter what noises you hear, don't aim the flashlight in any other direction but down."

Alicia was trembling as she reached out to hold Ronnie's hand. Once she found his hand and squeezed it, Alicia whispered, "Ronnie, how do you feel?"

Ronnie answered, "I'm doin' okay...but my ankle has swollen, so it's pretty tight in the boot."

Alicia moved her hand to Ronnie's cheek. "Shelley, Ronnie's starting to run a fever... We got to make it to the boat and get him some medicine."

Shelley came to her knees and laid the back of her hand against Ronnie's face. She said, "Alicia's right, you got a fever. We need to get back to the ship. Let's get a move on."

This time, it took Shelley and Alicia both to raise Ronnie to his feet. Each one of them placed one of Ronnie's arms around their necks and firmly gripped his wrists. Shelley had already secured the body bag to one of the backpacks straps so she could help support Ronnie and have a free hand for the flashlight. The trio began to take small, calculated steps in their quest for the landing area. By the second or third step, they heard the sound of whatever was above them in the woods start to shadow them as they moved. Shelley reminded Alicia that they had company and not to shine the light into the trees.

***

Whitney's entire body jerked as the gunshot sound made its way to the deck of the ship. Every head that had been staring at the area around the cabins from last year shifted at the same time. Nobody uttered a word until the high-pitched scream echoed through the bay. Whitney turned to Elaine and asked, "What just happened?"

Elaine never took her eyes off the darkness in the direction of the meadow. "I'm afraid that something bad just happened, Whitney."

"What about Ronnie, Shelley, and Alicia?" Whitney asked.

Rob answered, "Remember, they have weapons also. If they had been involved with whatever just took place, there would have been more than one gunshot."

Elaine turned to Captain Frank. "Better have the crew make some fresh coffee," she said. "Gonna be a long night."

CHAPTER 18

Brad Easton finally made it to the opening of the forest for the cabins. He scanned the road for any signs of activity. As Brad looked across the old cabins toward the bay, he could clearly see the lights of the ship and their reflection on the water. Even though he had some distance to cover, a small calmness came over Brad as he realized there was no dark forest between him and the bay. As he surveyed the clearing, Brad took note of the fact he had heard nothing around him. In fact, he had heard nothing since the howl from the mountain that Brad surmised came after something had happened to Jeff.

But the serene calmness was shattered when the gunshot from David's gun came rushing down the mountain and the scream echoed throughout the entire area. Brad slowly sank to his knees when he realized they were separated as a group and were now being hunted one at a time. He was sure of Joe's fate and had a pretty good idea about Jeff. He had no explanation of where the others in his group were, or what was taking place. All he knew for sure was that there was a single gunshot and a loud scream from the forest somewhere behind him. He felt totally alone at the edge of the clearing as Brad looked out over the clearing.

For a brief moment, Brad had a sensation of guilt run through his mind for moving down the road earlier, but had he known for sure that there was somebody still at the meadow, Brad would never have vacated the area. As the thoughts continued to run rampantly through his brain, Brad justified in his mind his actions when he started back down the road. He had to try and find the two men who had hastily taken off running. After a few more minutes, Brad decided it was now or never, and he began to inch his way down the road. With each step, he listened closely and kept a keen eye on his surroundings. Brad was uncomfortable with the fact of the grass and scrub bushes being too tall to get a clear picture of something hiding in them, but at least he was not completely surrounded by the trees of the forest. Even through the night vision goggles, Brad could only see the roadbed and the tall grass that bordered it. The only sound Brad could hear was the crunching sound made when his boots impacted the small gravels scattered along the road.

Out of the silence came the two small grunts somewhere below and in front of Brad. He stopped immediately and focused on the sounds. Brad suddenly had the feeling that it was now his turn to be hunted, but he was not going down without a fight. Brad slowly slid his finger down to the trigger mechanism of the rifle and clicked the safety of the gun to the fire position, and after a quick look around, Brad figured that having the high ground above the cabins might be to his advantage. Next, he maneuvered up the embankment bordering the road and began to sneak through the grass to the hill above the cabins. He was trying his best to dodge any of the scrub bushes and small saplings to prevent the sound of anything rubbing against his clothing as he moved along.

Then came another grunt from below the area where Brad departed the road. He paused and crouched down to listen for other activities around him. Next came what Brad could only assume was an expulsion of air from something very large. He reasoned it to be a sound of disgust, much like a human disapproving of some type of action they had just witnessed. For a moment, in his mind, Brad thought that just maybe he had avoided the inevitable confrontation with these creatures, especially when he heard the movement of something below the road that seemed to be going back in the direction of the meadow.

Brad continued to remain hidden in the grass for several minutes, listening close for other movements around him. Slowly, he started crawling on all fours as he inched his way toward the top of the hill behind the cabins. Brad was being extra careful in his movements while trying to keep a watchful eye out around him. Suddenly the rifle bumped into something lying on the ground, causing an odd sound that caught Brad's attention. As he looked down to the matted grass, a human skull came into focus in the goggles he was wearing. Little did Brad know, he had just located Sandy from last year. He scanned the ground and soon located the rest of the skeleton lying in front of him. Brad could only partially see the damage to the spine.

Brad silently moved around the skeleton and continued to move slowly through the grass in his effort to escape. Then, out of nowhere, one of the creatures came to a standing position just a couple of feet in front of Brad. In one complete movement, the creature covered the distance between it and Brad. Brad didn't have time to even get to his knees and assume a firing position. The creature pounded on Brad with both feet driving his body face first into the dirt. In an instant, the spine of the man snapped under the weight and impact of the blow. Many other bones were shattered as the weight of the creature bared down on Brad's body. His lungs expelled the last breath he had just taken as his body was compressed between the massive feet and the hard soil of the clearing.

All happened in a split second, and by the time Brad's mind realized that an attack was taking place, his body lay motionless in the dew-covered grass, probably not 10 feet from Sandy. The creature hovered over Brad's broken body for a few seconds until it was convinced there were no signs of life. Next, it turned toward the bay and grunted twice. This was followed by the two single grunts from the creatures below the road that had helped drive Brad up the hill. Once again, silence fell on the clearing around the cabins.

***

Darkness had come too quickly for Harold as he searched for Aaron. The gunshot from the direction of the meadow and the vocalizations had only added to the stress of the situation. Harold had been searching for what he guessed to be a little over an hour now. He was beginning to think that possibly Aaron wasn't even here around the homestead. But what about the fire poker and the blood on the broken piece of glass still clinging to the wooden frame? *No, Aaron had to be here somewhere,* he thought. Just as Harold started to make another turn in his grid-like search, he spotted a khaki back-pack lying in a section of grass that was pushed over. The closer that Harold got to the object, the more he came to grips with all that was lying there.

Harold knelt on one knee to observe the body and let out a deep sigh. He removed his own backpack and unzipped it to open the main compart-ment. Once he found the light camouflage jacket, Harold placed it over Aaron's head and upper torso. In the only way he knew possible, Harold secured the coat by tying the arms together around Aaron's body. Next, he hoisted the limp body over his left shoulder and picked up the rifle with his right hand. When Harold came to his feet, instantly he caught sight of the massive figure standing just outside the tree line beyond the homestead. Harold stood there motionless until the *whoop* came from the area where the road traveled beyond the old house. He shifted his stance and noticed the second massive stature of a creature looking directly back at him. Just as his eyes focused on the second creature, it turned, began to walk away, and disappeared after crossing a small rise in the old road. When Harold turned back to the first creature, he only got a glimpse of its back as the creature melted back into the cover of the forest.

Harold waited for a couple of seconds and then began his journey past the old house to the old, abandoned road. The trek was not easy, even with the night vision goggles. Aaron was a lot heavier than Harold had anticipated, and each step had become a struggle by the time he had reached the road. Harold stopped and rested on the dirt of the road after he respectfully laid Aaron's body in the grass. He realized that this was going to be a difficult task, but it was his responsibility to bring Aaron back to the ship.

***

The pain in Ronnie's ankle had all but rendered him helpless in aiding the girls with their effort in getting him down the shoreline. Even with the numerous pauses to rest in their quest of traveling down the shore, the women were gasping for air. Several times, they had stumbled and just barely prevented Ronnie from falling to the ground, and just like last year, whatever was flanking them would stop and wait for the trio to begin to move once again. All three knew exactly what was occurring in the darkness of the forest, but nobody dared to look into the trees.

In the next 30 minutes, the three of them probably stopped another 10 times. It was all that Alicia and Shelley could do to put one foot in front of the other while assisting Ronnie. Just a step or two from stopping to rest again, Shelley caught the toe of her boot on a piece of driftwood, and the three of them were thrown completely off balance and tumbled into the sandy soil of the shoreline. Ronnie winced in pain as he partially fell upon Alicia. Shelley fell face first into the dirt where her head collided with a baseball-sized rock lying on the shore. Alicia tried to maneuver out from under Ronnie, but she didn't have the strength to move his body. Shelley came to her knees and touched the bump already forming on her forehead. She could feel the wet substance against her fingers as she rubbed the spot. Once Shelley recovered her flashlight, she saw exactly what the wet substance was. Shelley's fingers were red with blood from the small cut at the impact spot. She then collapsed back to the ground exhausted, gasping for air. Alicia laid back onto the damp soil and shut her eyes; she too was trying to suck in as much air as possible in an effort to replenish her body.

Suddenly, there was movement in the woods above them, and it was drawing closer to where the three lay on the shoreline. They could clearly hear the edge of the bank, where the water met at high tide, giving way as the creature stepped onto the shoreline. Alicia still held the flashlight firmly in her hand but never moved it as the creature squatted beside her. She could feel its breath each time it exhaled, and the musky odor penetrated deep into her nostrils. Alicia had never experienced fear at this level before, but her body was so tired she knew there was nothing she could do. Shelley was still lying face down in the sandy soil. Ronnie was lying across Alicia, pinning her to the ground. In what little light there was, Alicia could barely make out the outline of the creature as it lifted Ronnie and started down the shoreline. She was too weak to stand on her feet, so Alicia simply crawled across the soil to Shelley. She fumbled around in the dark until she found Shelley's hand and squeezed it tightly, then a tear rolled off of Alicia's cheek. Next came a single shallow *whoop* from the direction that the creature had taken Ronnie. Once again, there was movement from the woods above the women coming down the hillside, and the second creature emerged from the trees.

Gently, the creature slid its massive hand through the soil underneath Alicia, and in one simple motion lifted her from the shoreline. Next, it was Shelley's turn to be hoisted off the damp ground. The best that Alicia could determine, they were being carried in the same direction as Ronnie. She found it odd, but Alicia continued to carry her flashlight aimed at the ground.

After several minutes, Alicia realized they were moving up a small embankment back into the trees. Suddenly they stopped, and the creature slowly eased her back onto the leaves. As Alicia bumped into Ronnie, she heard him moan in pain. Then she could hear what she imagined was Shelley being placed on the ground on the other side of Ronnie. Through pure exhaustion, Alicia released her grip on the flashlight, and it rolled off her fingertips and into the leaves shining back at her hand. Alicia saw the large hairy hand gently place the smooth round stone into the palm of her hand and disappear from the light. As Alicia gripped the rock, she heard the creatures moving through the leaves away from them. Soon there was only silence that surrounded the three people.

Alicia wasn't sure why they had been carried to this spot until she got enough strength to roll over and look through the trees. Down the bay, Alicia could see the lights of the boat and their reflection on the water. She crawled on her belly to the edge of the trees and began waving the light at the boat. She only hoped that someone was keeping an eye out for a signal to come and help.

Rob was the first to spot the light waving in the darkness. "There!" he said. "At the shoreline, that's a flashlight."

Everyone focused on the direction that Rob was pointing, and Whitney said, "I see it too...at the edge of the bay."

Captain Frank scurried to the ship's door and flung it open. "Come on, boys... We got us a pickup."

Immediately, the floodlights of the ship illuminated, and the crew jumped into action, grabbing their gear. Two of the young crew slid into the raft, and the one in back started the outboard motor. Within seconds, the raft was enroute to the trio at the shoreline. Alicia realized she had succeeded when the raft's motor came to life. After a couple of minutes, the driver of the raft slid it onto the shore after the crew spotted the trio with the spotlight. The crewman in front helped Alicia into the raft. Next he carried Ronnie and Shelley to the vessel, one at a time. With Alicia's help, it only took a matter of seconds to board Ronnie and Shelley. The driver reversed the engine and aimed the raft at the ship.

They pulled alongside the landing platform and secured the raft with ropes. More of the crew were standing there to assist with the unloading of the raft. As Shelley was helped onto the platform, one of the crew took her backpack along with the body bag that was fastened to it. The body bag was taken to the holding room for storage. All three were taken inside the ship, and Elaine quickly checked them out.

Alicia was in pretty good shape. Rest was the major thing she would require. Shelley would need a couple of stitches, but a good cleaning of the wound and some gauze would have to do for now. Elaine then administered some pain medicine to Ronnie and gave him an injection of antibiotics. The state of the ankle would have to be determined once they got back to the fishing village.

All three were made comfortable in the bunks of their cabin room. Elaine asked one of the crewmen to keep an eye on them while she returned to the deck. Just as she opened the door to the corridor, Alicia whispered her name, and Elaine turned to look at her. Alicia pulled the stone from her pocket and grinned as she displayed it to Elaine.

Elaine smiled. "Huh... Got you a stone."

Alicia looked at the rock in her hand. "Yeah... Now I know how you felt when the mother gave the stone to you. But I'm not gonna lie, Elaine. I was scared to death."

Elaine replied, "Don't tell anyone, but so was I."

Alicia laid her head on the pillow as Elaine exited the room. With the smooth, round stone clutched firmly in hand, Alicia faded off to sleep.

CHAPTER 19

The journey back up the old road was beginning to take a toll on Harold. It had now been several hours since he discovered Aaron's body and began the task of bringing him back. Each time Harold would stop to take a break, the effort of lifting the body to resume the trek had grown more and more difficult, but he was determined to return Aaron to the ship. As Harold rested this time on both knees in the dirt of the road, his thoughts ran back to the moment he first stood with Aaron on his shoulder back at the homestead.

Why were the creatures just watching them from a distance? Why did they disappear beyond the road and into the trees? Were these the creatures responsible for Aaron's death, and why didn't they attack him also? Why had he heard nothing in the woods around him as he moved up the road? As a matter of fact, why were there no sounds around him at all?

Once Harold's breathing subsided enough and his body had somewhat recovered, he slowly placed Aaron's body over his shoulder. It was all he could do to get to his feet. Harold looked down at the road and noticed the rifle lying on the dirt beside his feet. He contemplated for just a second how he was going to achieve the task of picking it up while trying to support Aaron and himself. Then, Harold decided he hadn't needed the weapon so far, and it wasn't worth the effort to retrieve the rifle. If something did happen, Harold knew he didn't have the strength to ward off an attack anyway.

Harold raised his head and took a quick look up the road with the night vision goggles; it was time to continue the journey to the landing zone.

Each step was a move in the right direction, but they were becoming more difficult as Harold stumbled along. He couldn't remember ever being this exhausted in his life. Suddenly, Harold's right foot landed on a large limb lying on the road. As the weight of the two men shifted to that side, Harold's boot rolled off the limb and his knee buckled in the effort to support them. He did his best to protect Aaron as the two of them plummeted toward the ground. Harold collided with the dirt face first and came to rest with Aaron's body partially lying on top of him. As Harold lay there, he wasn't sure that he would be able to even get back to his feet again, and getting Aaron across his shoulder seemed like an impossible task in his mind.

Suddenly, Harold began to smell a musky odor that started to surround him, and then he heard something walking up the road from behind them. The thought of the rifle he left behind crossed Harold's mind. As he took a deep breath and exhaled the air, Harold could feel the tiny dirt particles suck into his nose and exit his body. He knew at this moment that his mind and body had given in to whatever was about to take place.

The first thing that Harold felt was the weight of Aaron's body being lifted off of him, and next was the pressure of the backpack straps upon his chest as he himself was lifted off the road. Harold didn't have the strength or the mental capacity to do anything about the actions taking place; he was now purely along for the ride. Harold could feel the creature taking a couple of steps up the road and turning down into the forest. It continued to carry the two men through the darkness of the trees—to where, Harold had no idea.

***

Wilson had been sitting patiently in his hiding spot for a few hours now. Nothing had come up or down the road. The night had become deathly quiet, and Wilson was growing more impatient with the passing of each minute. Suddenly he heard something approaching from below the old road. The sound of crunching leaves and the occasional sound of something colliding with one of the small saplings told Wilson that whatever it was, it was very large. He clicked the safety of the rifle to the fire position and readied himself for the moment, but the moment never came. Wilson listened to whatever was moving in the darkness below him as it navigated past him, moving in an angle toward the bay. He could never catch a glimpse of it because of the lower edge of the road blocking his view. Harold could only sit and listen as the creature made its way down the hillside toward the bay in front of the cabins. Just maybe the creature was moving to the spot that he and David had thought they saw something with their spotlights from the ship. Wilson could not confirm that what he had heard was indeed one of the creatures. He had no earthly idea that this particular individual was returning Harold and Aaron to the landing zone.

Wilson did realize that, shortly, daylight would be coming to the port, and perhaps he could intercept the movement of a creature as it traveled past the cabins to the hill behind them. He and David were sure that the creatures they spotted were watching the ship. They must have climbed the hill just before daybreak to remain out of sight. Wilson decided to leave the hunting spot and make a move for the cabins. Once he gathered his gear and readied his backpack, Wilson stepped out of the trees and started up the road. The eyes watching from behind his position took note of his movement. The creature began to stealthily travel from the mountain in the direction of the hill behind the cabins. Wilson had no idea he was being observed while he was watching the old road.

After about an hour of slipping up the road without as much as a detectable sound, Wilson spotted the break in the forest that told him he was at the clearing for the cabins. Now, he needed to find his next hiding spot quickly before any more time passed. The creatures should be moving past the cabins to the safety of the forest soon. Carefully, Wilson began to sneak along the dirt of the road until the cabins from last year came into view. He paused for a minute to scan the area for any signs of movement or danger, and after feeling secure that he was alone, Wilson decided his best option for spotting one of these things was probably from a position on one of the cabin decks. Methodically, Wilson made his way from the road to the path that led to the cabins, and he paused for just a second to listen before climbing the steps of the crew cabin.

After hearing no sounds around him, Wilson eased up the wooden planks that the steps were constructed of one at a time. As he reached the top of the stairs, Wilson once again paused and stared through the opening where the door once stood, trying to determine where the best possible hunting spot would be. It didn't take long for Wilson to come to a decision on the situation. He needed to be on the outside of the cabin to hear all that was happening in the foliage around the structures.

Wilson slowly made his way around the corner of the crew cabin and faced the contestant cabin from last year. All was still eerily quiet from the entire area around the cabins. Wilson hugged the wall as he made his way almost to the end of the deck. He lowered himself to sit with his back against the wall. Wilson could see over the railing to catch any movement above the cabins and through the spindles of the railing for anything closely around him. This was the best possible spot for the rest of the night's hunt, and Wilson settled in. He had no idea that each and every movement of his was being monitored by several sets of eyes surrounding him.

***

Everyone was still standing on the bow of the ship as daybreak began to creep into the bay. Captain Frank was the first to notice as he stared through the light fog dancing across the water. The captain released his grip on the ships railing and pointed. "There, at the landing zone. Looks like two people on the shoreline."

Captain Frank once again banged on the side of the ship with his fist as he opened the door. He leaned his head through the opening and shouted, "Come on, boys! We got us another pickup."

Elaine, Rob, and Whitney squeezed by the captain on their way to the launching pad for the raft. Captain Frank turned and said, "Just where are you three going?"

Elaine answered without even looking around, "We're going to help."

Captain Frank shrugged and closed the door to follow; within a matter of seconds, they were on the platform along with the two young crew members to operate the raft. After the boys slid into the vessel, they assisted the other three into their spots and the outboard engine came to life. Captain Frank pivoted for his return to the bow to watch the recovery process.

Slowly, as Harold began to regain consciousness, he realized the noise approaching him was the whine of a motor, and Harold felt the sensation of his hand being clinched tightly into a fist. He could feel the smooth, round object as it pressed against his palm with the pressure applied by his fingers. Harold began to raise himself in the sandy soil of the shoreline by pushing up with both fists. The raft slid onto the shore, and immediately all but the driver hopped out. They quickly realized only one of the two men were alive.

Elaine placed her hand on Harold's shoulder. "Where's your radio?"

Harold simply pointed at the pack he still wore. Elaine unzipped the pack and started searching for the device. At the exact same moment, Shelley exited the door of the ship, found Captain Frank, and made her way to the bow of the ship. She reached out and touched the captain's shoulder. "What's going on?" she asked.

Captain Frank answered, "Looks like we got a couple more people to pick up."

Shelley turned to the shore. "Alive?"

Captain Frank tilted his head and replied, "Not sure yet."

After watching the activity on the shore for a few seconds, Shelley took a quick look around the area of the cabins. Out of sheer luck, she spotted an odd color lying in the grass on the hill. Shelley asked the captain for his binoculars, and as she took a closer look, Shelley could make out something of a red color protruding from the grass. She tapped the captain on the arm with the glasses and said, "On the hill behind the cabins, there's something red lying in the grass."

Captain Frank took the binoculars from Shelley's hand and began to search as she guided his efforts. Once he found the object, the captain studied it closely. "That looks like a backpack, Shelley. Whatever it is, it doesn't belong there."

Elaine turned the knob on the radio to *on* and pressed the key button. "Captain Frank, this is Elaine... Do you copy?"

The captain was startled a little when Elaine's voice blasted through the device: "Loud and clear, Elaine."

Elaine pressed the *talk* button again. "We got Harold...and Aaron, unfortunately. Aaron did not survive, Captain."

Shelley grabbed the radio. "Elaine, up on the hill above the cabins... There's something lying in the grass."

Elaine looked at the others and once again pushed the button. "Can you guide me to it?"

Shelley responded, "Yes. When you get the two of them here, I'll go back on the raft with you."

Rob shook his head no. "You tell her that you and I will check it out," he said. "She can direct us over the radio."

They loaded Aaron onto the raft and assisted Harold into the vessel. The young crewman turned to take Whitney's hand, and she smiled. "No thanks," she said. "I'm going with them."

Elaine looked into Whitney's eyes. "You really don't—"

Whitney interrupted, "Let's see what's on that hill."

The young crewman handed Rob another body bag as he stood on the shore at the bow of the raft, then he pushed their transportation off of the shore until it floated freely in the water of the bay. Elaine radioed Shelley back on the boat and gave her the information as Rob had instructed. The only thing she added was that Whitney would be accompanying them. The next thing the three individuals knew, they were climbing the path to the cabins. Right away, all three noticed the odor that surrounded them.

***

Wilson clearly heard the outboard motor as it fired and made its way to the shore. He had observed the number of people in it and the occupants when the raft returned to the ship. Wilson knew that there was someone somewhere because of the smaller number of people in the raft as it returned to the ship. Wilson turned to start the hunt once again. He knew from the odor in the air that he had made the right decision when he moved to the cabins.

***

Elaine, Rob, and Whitney were standing beside the crew cabin by the time the young boys assisted Harold onto the landing platform. Elaine keyed the radio and asked Shelley if she had eyes on them. Shelley responded with an affirmative and informed the group that she would guide them to the spot. As Elaine turned to start for the old road, her eyes caught the objects lying on the railing of the cabin adjacent to the window facing them. Now, there were three stones placed side by side on the plank board. Elaine paused for just a second as she studied the rocks.

Rob whispered, "What's wrong, Elaine?"

Elaine answered in a normal speaking volume, "On the railing...the three stones."

Rob and Whitney both focused on the rocks, then Elaine added, "There's still one person besides us left on this shore... Oh, and I don't think there's really any need to whisper now, guys. These things are right here. That's evident from the smell in the air. We know they are here, and they know we are here."

A shiver ran up Whitneys back. "Are we sure this is something we should be doing?"

Elaine answered, "I believe so... They could have already made their move if they wanted to, Whitney. I believe we will be okay."

Rob said, still whispering, "How do you know there is another person other than us on the shore?"

Elaine finally moved her eyes from the stones to look at Rob. "There are three rocks on the railing, and I already have mine. Two of the stones, I think, may be for you and Whitney."

Rob turned to Whitney and then back to Elaine. He said, "Maybe the third one is for Alicia or Harold."

Elaine grinned. "Alicia showed me the rock she received, and I noticed that Harold never opened one of his hands down at the loading zone. I think he was holding his rock tightly inside the fist he was making."

Elaine turned to face the old road and took a deep breath. She nodded and said, "Let's go." As she started to walk, Whitney and Rob fell into line, with Whitney assuming the middle position. Several pairs of eyes watched as they began the trek to the red object.

CHAPTER 20

The trek up the road was a fairly easy walk consisting of a few switch-backs and the occasional object to maneuver around. The odor in the air around the group remained consistent as they moved along. Elaine and Shelley remained in contact periodically as the three hiked the road. Shelley wanted the three to know they were not alone in their efforts. The only moments that produced an uneasy feeling for Shelley were when the foliage would block her view of the group. In just a few more feet, they would have to leave the comforts of the road and venture up into the tall grass.

Shelley pushed the button on the radio and said, "Okay, guys... You need to start up the hill right there."

Elaine came to a halt and lifted the radio to her head. "Roger that, Shelley. Here we go."

The three of them climbed the small bank bordering the road and began to navigate the tall grass. Intermittently, Shelley's voice emerged from the radio and told them to move a little to the right or left. There was hardly anything that the three of them could make out in the tall grass around them, but Shelley was not the only one watching them.

From his crouched position on the deck, Wilson had been observing the three moving up the road and into the clearing. Several yards to their right and slightly above the group was a dark spot behind one of the many scrub bushes that littered the hillside that Wilson had been watching for a while.

Just as Shelley radioed that the object was directly in front of them, Elaine caught sight of the backpack. Another step and she had a full view of the scene in front of them. Elaine dropped her head as Whitney stepped up next to her. Whitney let out a small gasp and turned her head to look away. Rob placed a hand on each of Whitney's shoulders and guided her to the right. Whitney responded by taking a few steps and kneeling on both knees down into the grass.

Elaine said, "Brad Easton..."

Rob simply replied, "Yeah."

Elaine turned to face the boat and lifted the radio to her face. "Shelley, you guys were right. It's Brad Easton. We'll get him in the bag and start back."

"Roger that," Shelley said.

"You guys don't see anything else?" Elaine asked.

Shelley said, "Like what?"

Elaine answered, "Keep an eye out... I think there's one person besides us around here."

Rob started to unfold the bag, and Whitney started to stand. Her eyes caught something lying almost hidden under the grass. She said, "People... There's another person here."

Elaine moved to Whitney's side and caught sight of the cross-training shoes protruding beneath the blades of grass. Right away, she recognized them. She said, "Sandy... She almost made it to the cabins."

Rob stepped up beside the women and sighed, "We'll put Sandy in the bag, and I will carry Brad over my shoulder."

It took several minutes, but the group was able to recover Sandy's remains and place her in the bag. Rob covered Brad the best he could with a jacket from his backpack, and the three started down the road. Wilson watched the group all the way down the hill until the back of the cabin blocked his view, and he turned to scan the hillside. As his eyes came to the bush with the dark spot behind it, Wilson saw the creature standing on two feet staring back at him. Immediately it dropped back down into the grass and started moving away from the hill. Wilson tried desperately to draw a bead on the creature as it moved, but all he could see was the tops of the grass swaying from side to side.

Just as the three of them started to pass the cabins, Elaine's radio came to life and Shelley whispered through the device, "Elaine, I think I just saw a movement on the other side of the crew cabin. Pretty sure I saw a hand and the end of a rifle moving at the deck's railing."

The three people came to a dead stop. Elaine nodded for her and Whitney to set the body bag down. Rob followed suit with Brad's body, then the three of them made their way to the steps of the cabin and quietly climbed the wooden planks. Elaine eased to the corner of the cabin and peeped around it; she spotted Wilson looking through the scope of the rifle, searching for a target. Elaine slipped down the side of the cabin until she heard Wilson click the safety of the firearm to the fire position, and she lunged forward and folded her arms against her chest. She collided with Wilson from the back and sent him face first into the railing of the deck.

As Wilson fell, he aimlessly pulled the trigger and fired the gun into the crisp blue sky. Wilson was the first of the two to regain their composure and get back to his feet. Then, he turned to Elaine just as she came to her feet and slammed the butt of the rifle into her chest. The blow sent Elaine tumbling backwards until her feet could no longer keep pace with her body, and Elaine finally lost her balance and fell onto the wooden planks of the deck.

Just as Rob positioned his hands under Elaine's armpits to lift her up, the massive figure glided over the deck's railing. The creature's feet impacted the deck with a loud thud. Wilson tried to swing around, but it was much too late. The muscular arms wrapped around Wilson and began to apply pressure. The creature lifted Wilson's feet off the deck just as Rob helped Elaine back to her feet, and the three people all stared in amazement as the pressure began to exhibit itself on Wilson's face.

As Elaine continued to watch the event unfold, something suddenly caught her attention... Down between the shoulder and the elbow of the creature was a calloused scar that had no hair growth on it. Elaine once again made eye contact with the creature. It was staring back at only her. She smiled slightly as she realized that this was the juvenile she had administered first aid to last year. It had grown into a mighty, young but mature adult. Slowly, she moved away from Rob and approached the mighty creature.

Rob and Whitney remained motionless as Elaine reached out and touched the scar with her hand. The creature only blinked as it held Wilson tightly in its grip. Elaine lowered her hand and addressed Wilson, "Ironic isn't it, Wilson? The creature you came here to kill is now gonna kill you."

Elaine turned and walked away. As she passed Rob and Whitney, she simply told them to come on. As the trio started down the steps, they could clearly hear Wilson's body giving way under the immense pressure applied by the creature. When they reached the path between the cabins, they heard a *thump* sound as Wilson's body fell to the wooden planks. When the three of them started up the path, another creature stepped out from the upper side of the cabin. Elaine wasn't totally sure, but she had the feeling that this was the mother from a year ago.

The creature approached the three people and extended a hand to Whitney. Elaine instructed Whitney to take the gift. Then, the creature placed the smooth, round stone in Whitney's palm, and the gesture was repeated with Rob. It reached out to Elaine, but this time the creature stretched forth its hand with its palm up. Elaine placed her hand into the palm of the creature's hand, and slowly it stroked Elaine's hand with its thumb for a few seconds and withdrew the arm. The creature turned and walked away. As it walked past the edge of the cabin, another juvenile appeared from beneath the deck and took the mother's hand. Together they made their way to the old road and disappeared into the forest.

Elaine looked at the railing of the deck one more time. There were no more stones lying on the wooden plank. The three of them gathered Brad and Sandy to begin heading for the landing area.

***

Soon, the raft was secured, and all were safely on the ship. Brad and Sandy were placed in the holding room. The captain ordered the young crew to start the engines and ready the ship for the return to the fishing village. Within a matter of minutes, the ship began to slowly move out of the port. Elaine remained on the deck, hoping to get one more glimpse of the young creature that had grown into the massive figure she had witnessed at the cabin. Just as the boat began to glide by the large rock she had seen the mother and juvenile on last year, the creature emerged from the trees. Elaine held out her arm, and the creature mimicked the gesture. As it dropped its arm, the Hairy Man of Port Chatham arched its back and released a bellowing howl that echoed throughout the port. Then, the creature turned and disappeared into the forest. Elaine returned into the interior of the ship after taking in one last view of the bay and its surroundings.

As Elaine walked past Captain Frank, they exchanged winks. She walked down the narrow corridor and entered their quarters. Ronnie was sitting on the side of his bunk with Alicia by his side. The swelling in his ankle appeared to be subsiding a little. Rob was lying on his bunk with his eyes shut, and Whitney was rotating the stone given to her with the tips of her fingers, much like a child studying a bright, shiny object they had just received as a gift. Everyone settled in for the voyage back to the fishing village. Not a word was spoken.

After an X-ray of Ronnie's ankle had proven that indeed it was just a bad sprain, the group enjoyed a hearty meal at the village, and all were able to take a much-needed shower. Everyone turned in for a good night's rest, and this time nobody so much as moved in the sleeping bags provided for them. When daylight came once again, Captain Frank roused the people from their bunks. After a nice breakfast, everybody began to load into the vans for the trip to the airport.

Elaine walked over to Captain Frank and wrapped both arms around him. She could already smell the special sauce on his breath. She poked the captain on the chest with her index finger. "Better back off the sauce a little, Captain."

Captain Frank grinned. "That's the reason I don't go to doctors, little lady."

Elaine laughed and climbed into the van. The driver started the engine, and in no time at all they were on the small road. The ride was relatively quiet except when Ronnie would groan slightly as the van encountered a pothole or ran over a bump in the road. Mostly everyone just sat and took in the scenery as they rode along. At the airport, the staff assisted Ronnie on the plane. Alicia carried both her and Ronnie's gear as they walked into the facility. Conley took one of the bags from Alicia and carried it to the plane. It was at that moment that Elaine and Shelley noticed that Rob was not carrying any gear.

Elaine looked at Rob. "Hey... Where's your gear?"

Rob smiled. "Gonna hang around for a while, Elaine. I might just enjoy the simple way of life for a spell."

Elaine tilted her head. "May not be so simple, Rob. These people work hard up here. And by the way... I don't see a major network around here."

Rob chuckled, "I wanna see if this is the life for me. It might just be my cup of tea... Plus, I can keep a closer watch on the creatures of the port from here. Captain Frank and Conley said they could get me some employment and help in any way possible, so I'm gonna stick around and make a go of it, for a while anyway."

Elaine hugged Rob and turned to Whitney. "Ready to go?"

Whitney smiled from ear to ear and said, "I'm staying, too. Somebody's got to keep an eye on Rob."

Elaine smiled. "Good for you two. Hang in there, and good luck, guys."

Elaine started to board the plane but paused to look back at Rob and Whitney, who were walking back to the hangar building. Elaine said, "Hey, Rob?"

The two stopped and turned to Elaine, then Elaine pointed at Rob. "Don't call us... We'll call you."

Rob laughed out loud as Elaine turned and entered the plane's door. The two of them watched through the large plate glass window as the plane took off and disappeared into the vast skies of Alaska.

ACKNOWLEDGMENTS

I would once again like to thank my wife, Tammy, for her encouragement in the writing of the book. I would also like to thank everyone who read *The Breath of Darkness.* I appreciate all the feedback from everyone.

Don't Miss the Next Book!

We see things we cannot explain. We have nightmares about beings that are not real. But for the people pursuing this creature from a time that has long passed, its existence is something that none of them ever dreamt to be possible. Just maybe, some dreams are more real than we ever imagined.

www.ingramcontent.com/pod-product-compliance
Lightning Source LLC
Chambersburg PA
CBHW060646260626
47161CB00008B/3020